THE DAY WE SAVED THE FUTURE

**ALSO BY ASHLEY
AND JORDAN BANJO,
IN COLLABORATION WITH
ALEXANDRA SHEPPARD:**

THE DAY WE SAVED THE FUTURE

ASHLEY BANJO   JORDAN BANJO

WITH ALEXANDRA SHEPPARD

ILLUSTRATED BY BRITTNEY BOND

■SCHOLASTIC

Published in the UK by Scholastic, 2023
1 London Bridge, London, SE1 9G
Scholastic Ireland, 89E Lagan Road, Dublin Industrial Estate,
Glasnevin, Dublin, D11 HP5F

SCHOLASTIC and associated logos are trademarks and/or
registered trademarks of Scholastic Inc.

Text © Ashley Banjo and Jordan Banjo, 2023
Illustrations by Brittney Bond © Scholastic, 2023

The right of Ashley Banjo and Jordan Banjo to be identified as the
authors of this work has been asserted by them under the
Copyright, Designs and Patents Act 1988.

ISBN 978 0702 30645 7

A CIP catalogue record for this book
is available from the British Library.

Printed by CPI Group (UK) Ltd, Croydon, CR0 4YY
Paper made from wood grown in sustainable forests
and other controlled sources.

1 3 5 7 9 10 8 6 4 2

This is a work of fiction. Names, characters, places, incidents
and dialogues are products of the author's imagination or are used
fictitiously. Any resemblance to actual people, living or dead,
events or locales is entirely coincidental.

www.scholastic.co.uk

FOR OUR KIDS:
CASS, MICAH,
MIMI AND ROSE

PROLOGUE

THE FUTURE – 2045

A ramshackle car speeds out of a tunnel in the ground at lightning speed. With its rusty doors and mismatched wheels it doesn't look as though it would survive the miles it's clocking up. But it hurtles along the empty London roads, past abandoned skyscrapers that once stood proud and shining. The only source of light for miles around comes from the car's wonky headlamps. Electricity is restricted at this time of night.

In a high-tech underground garage, two engineers huddle over a screen. They watch the car's dashcam in tense silence. This is one journey they can't go on. They are forced to observe from afar.

"Are you confident the wheels are bolted on securely, bro?"

"For the last time, Cass, yes! I triple-checked," Micah says. "Those wheels are secured tighter than Dad's wallet used to be on pocket money day."

The driverless car picks up speed and momentum, turning corners with ease. Suddenly, a computerized voice bleeps inside the car and rings through the underground garage's speakers.

"PURSUER DETECTED. PURSUER DETECTED."

The brothers look at each other, confused.

"Must be an error. There isn't a single car in

a thousand-mile radius that can keep up with Frank," Cass says.

A crackle pipes up on the speakers. *"Er, fellas. Looks like I've got company. Check for yourselves!"*

"Frank, can you show us the rear-view camera?" Micah asks.

On the screen they see another car. The blood chills in their veins. Sleek, silver and speeding up. There's no doubt about it: a beast of a supercar is chasing Frank.

Micah gulps. "There can only be one person behind this."

Cass shakes his head. "Impossible. They don't have this technology!"

"Now ain't the time for bickering!" Frank says. *"You need to get me out of this mess, and fast!"*

"Increase the speed immediately," Cass says.

"Right-o, boss!" Frank says.

The speedometer levels on the screen increase well into the hundreds.

"I estimate Frank will be at the pier in approximately three minutes. The wormhole will be open and ready for him," Cass says.

Micah pays close attention to the rear-view camera. The supercar is just a few metres behind Frank.

Then something weird happens. As Micah and Cass watch on the screen, the supercar's bonnet slowly lifts up to reveal what look like … mini cannons.

An almighty CRACK booms through the speakers.

"Whoa!" Micah yells.

Frank's rear windshield explodes; shards of glass shatter on to the pavement and the car's patchwork interior. The supercar rains iron-coated rubber bullets on to Frank, ripping holes through the car's bumper.

"What is going on here?" says Cass.

"They're blowing up our only chance at

saving the world, that's what's going on!" Micah hisses.

"Fellas, if we don't do something I'm gonna be more colander than car!" Frank yells.

"The wormhole is ready. Just hold on! The docks are only one mile away!" Cass says, trying to collect himself. This was not part of the plan.

Sure enough, the camera on Frank's front dashboard shows dark water up ahead.

An awful screeching sound fills the speakers.

"You hear that? It's my bumper dragging on the road. I'm not gonna make it!" Frank yells.

"Keep going, Frank! You've got this!" Micah yells back.

"If only we had real car parts instead of scrap metal," Cass mutters. "Frank's barely begun his mission and he's already a mess!"

"You know we had to get creative. Steel and rubber is strictly rationed. Just like everything else in this city," Micah says darkly. "Frank might not be the fanciest car on the road, but his engine is sound."

The supercar is now neck-and-neck with Frank. It swerves into the ramshackle car, trying to bully him into the water. Grey smoke flares from the road and the stink of burnt rubber fills the air.

"We've got to lose the mystery supercar!" Micah yells. "Frank is our only shot at—"

"I know," says Cass, trying to stay calm. "Frank, I need you to listen carefully: activate Camo Mode."

"Boss, are you sure? It'll drain my battery!"

Micah and Cass look at each other. It's risky – but what choice do they have?

Suddenly, the supercar swerves into Frank so hard that the car goes into a wild tailspin.

"Camo Mode it is!" Frank yells.

And, just like that, Frank disappears. The beams from the headlights vanish, the engine goes silent and Frank's rough exterior transforms into a sleek reflective surface that blends into the darkness. The supercar brakes, as if confused, while Frank speeds off silently and invisibly towards the pier.

"Well done, mate!" yells Micah, punching the air. "I've input the wormhole's coordinates into your GPS. Can you see it up ahead?"

The wormhole comes into view at the end of the pier, a silent swirling bubble in the night sky.

"Got it!" Frank says.

"Remember, you need to reach two hundred and twenty-two miles per hour to activate the time travel protocol," Micah says. "Otherwise you'll land in the water and it's game over!"

The car gathers momentum, but Cass shakes his head. "Frank isn't picking up enough speed."

"I've gotta switch off Camo Mode, fellas!" Frank yells. *"It's slowing me down."*

"But they'll see you!" Micah says.

"Frank's right. It must be deactivated – it's the only way the car will make it through the wormhole," Cass says. "Do it, Frank. Wait until you hit the pier."

"Got it." Frank reaches the pier and flickers into view. Once again, the engine revs and the headlights sweep the darkness. Like a predator that has sniffed out its prey, the supercar chases Frank down the pier.

"See you on the other side, lads!" Frank yells before the sound from the speaker dissolves into white noise. He flies off the end of the pier and into the swirling wormhole.

The brothers watch with bated breath.

"Did he make it?" says Cass, scanning the screen.

"Looks like it," says Micah.

"Wait, where did that supercar go?" Cass asks.

"Who cares?" says Micah, with a sigh of relief. "If Frank made it, our work here is done."

"I guess," says Cass, frowning at the screen. He shakes his head. "Yes, I suppose you're right. We've done everything we can. Let's just hope the boys can handle it from here."

The brothers sit back in their underground garage and look at each other. *Have they done enough*?

What they didn't see, was what followed Frank through the wormhole.

The supercar.

1

2023

"Yo, Micah! Wait for me!"

Micah stopped in his tracks and sighed. He'd thought he could slip out of the house a few minutes early and avoid his little bro tagging along with him to school.

No such luck.

"Mum said you've got to walk with me," Cass puffed, running up behind him. The sleeves of his too-big blazer hanging out from his winter coat.

Mum waved at them from the doorstep, her

fluffy dressing gown wrapped tight against the October chill. "Look after him, Micah! And don't forget Aunty Joanne is coming round for tea tonight. She's looking forward to seeing you both," she said.

The boys both sighed at the thought of Aunty Joanne coming over – she was so boring!

"Bro, you started school at the same time as me," Micah muttered. "Don't you know the way yet?"

"What's the big deal? We're heading to the same place anyway."

No need to remind me, Micah thought.

Same school. Same year group. Same classroom.

Yep. Thanks to Cass's "superb academic performance" he had been boosted up a year. He had skipped Year 6 altogether, landing him straight into Year 7 alongside Micah.

His little brother in *his* class.

The brothers shared bunk beds and now they shared a school timetable.

Just perfect. It seemed to Micah like his little bro was constantly trailing after him.

Their route to school took them down Stratford High Street, which was busier than ever on a Friday morning. The queue for the bus stop stretched past several shops and was full of grown-ups wearing suits and clutching steaming hot coffee cups. The smell from the new bakery, with its trays of French pastries in the window, mingled with the exhaust fumes from the rush hour traffic.

"Try to memorize the way, Cass," Micah said. "It's easy! We just walk down the high street and turn right at that old boarded-up building with the steps and fancy pillars."

Cass nodded. He would never admit it to Micah, but he felt intimidated by the crowds of older teenagers and grown-ups clogging the

pavement. His old primary school was only two minutes from their house. He could do that walk backwards with his eyes closed.

There was one thing that Cass preferred about this walk to school, and that was the corner shop. He and Micah had stopped by every morning for fifty pence worth of fizzy cola bottles that they ate on their way to school. The shop door creaked as the boys pushed it open, letting in a gust of cold air.

"Morning, Mrs Khan! We'll have the usual, please," Micah said to the elderly lady behind the counter.

Mrs Khan chuckled. "Do your mum and dad know you're having pure sugar for breakfast?"

"I won't tell if you won't," Micah smiled. The brothers had known The Khans, the couple who owned the shop, as long as he could remember. Mr Khan used to train at Poppa's boxing gym.

They left the shop with a small paper bag of

sweets. They had to be eaten quickly; sweets were strictly banned at Eastbrook Secondary.

"Oh, Dad wanted me to remind you about extra boxing lessons after school tonight. He reckons you need to practise your right hook," Cass said while chewing a cola bottle.

Micah rolled his eyes. Cass didn't know how lucky he was. For some reason, Dad was convinced that Micah was set to become the next boxing legend. Cass would start training when he turned eleven, and Micah hoped that would take some of the focus away from him. But Cass's eleventh birthday was a whole year away. Until then, Dad would only be on *his* case.

"I already told Dad I'm busy on Fridays," Micah said. "I've got to work on my science project."

"Wait a second, we have science homework? I don't remember Mrs Ashford saying anything about—"

"It's not a *school* science project," Micah mumbled, speeding up.

"Ohhh. You mean your car designs?" Cass asked, trotting alongside.

Micah scowled at his brother. "Say it a bit louder, Cass. I think there's a remote village in Norway that didn't quite hear you."

"You've got nothing to be embarrassed about, bro," Cass said, pushing his glasses up his nose. "Your engine designs are sick! If I could draw like you, I would share it with the world."

Even though he was too embarrassed to share his drawings with anyone except Cass, Micah broke into a smile just hearing about his favourite hobby.

Micah loved cars. Think about something you really love and multiply it by one thousand. *That* is how much Micah loved cars. He'd been obsessed with cars for as long as he could remember – from the age of four he could guess the make and model of a car from the headlamp alone – it was quite the party trick.

Micah loved the smell of cars. He loved their speed. But most of all, he loved to figure out ways to make them even cooler.

He had notebook after notebook filled with designs for souped-up cars: cars designed with automated parking, solar roof panels and remote driving technology. He was just as obsessed with the engines as he was with the tyres and paintwork.

For his tenth birthday, Micah's mum and dad took him to his uncle's mechanic's garage and let him help out for the afternoon. He came home covered in engine oil and the smell didn't leave his fingers for days.

It was the best birthday *ever*.

No one at school knew about Micah's obsession. He kept his sketches and designs hidden. His mates thought drawing was for little kids. They wouldn't get it.

And neither did Dad. He was a volunteer boxing coach at the local community centre and was determined Micah would follow in his family's footsteps.

See, Dad had it all planned out. Micah was to devote every non-school hour to boxing. Just like he had done, and his father before him.

"Three generations of boxers in this family," Dad said every Sunday during breakfast, as he sat under the portrait of their grandpa on the kitchen wall.

Poppa won the Olympic Gold medal for boxing. It didn't matter that Poppa died before Micah was born: the rest of the family would never forget his legacy.

Giant portraits of Poppa proudly holding his Olympic medal hung in every single room at home. The small living room was made even more cramped by a trophy cabinet that held all the boxing belts and awards. Micah's dad had been boxing since he was sixteen, and he was keen for his sons to continue the legacy. Micah had yet to earn a single medal, but that didn't deter Dad. Micah just needed more practice, he said. So he had to train every Friday night.

Micah loved that boxing made his dad so happy. His face lit up whenever Micah stepped into the ring.

There was only one problem: Micah didn't care about boxing. He didn't hate it; he was all right at it, but it just didn't make him happy in the same way cars did. Would Dad ever understand that? And would Micah ever gather the courage to tell him?

Click-Click-Click.

An annoying sound broke Micah out of his thoughts. "What on earth is that?" he asked, glancing at his brother.

Now that he had finished his fizzy cola bottles, Cass was completely focused on a brightly coloured cube-shaped toy, rotating the sides. He didn't play games on his phone or a console like a normal ten-year-old, oh no. He preferred puzzles and video games from the Stone Age rather than those with slick graphic design and hyper-realistic sound effects. While most kids would gladly do a month of extra chores for the latest virtual reality game, Cass was happier with something ancient and retro.

Micah thought it was kinda weird. And so would the other kids at school if they found out.

"It's a Rubik's Cube! Dad found it in the attic," Cass said excitedly. "It was his from the '80s."

"Yeah, and it should stay there," Micah said sternly. "You should be trying to make friends and fit in, not messing about with old-fashioned toys no one understands."

Cass shrugged, his eyes still locked on the

cube. He loved logic games nearly as much as Micah loved cars. He was a real brainbox – one of those people who was annoyingly good at everything. But his real passion was for astronomy (he asked for a telescope last Christmas) and algebra. Micah couldn't understand how someone could get excited about numbers until Cass explained that his beloved cars would be nothing more than scrap metal without mathematical equations.

He continued rotating the coloured cube. "It's not a toy, it's a mind game. And so what if—"

"All right, Micah," a voice interrupted. It was Jamie and a couple of other boys from their year. They weren't the nicest of kids, Micah had to admit, but hanging out with them meant that at least he didn't have to sit alone at lunch.

Jamie looked down at Cass, who was clicking away on his Rubik's Cube. "I didn't know they allowed toddlers into Eastbrook Secondary," he sneered.

"Yeah, are you lost, little boy?" Rav asked meanly. "The nursery's across the road."

Cass's cheeks flushed pink. He slipped the Rubik's Cube into his coat pocket.

"Let's go, Cass," Micah muttered, trying to pretend he hadn't noticed. "We're gonna be late."

"See you at lunch, yeah?" Jamie said to Micah. "But lose the pipsqueak."

Micah felt a little guilty about not standing up for Cass, but he had to learn not to be so … weird.

"I told you about that game," Micah said as they walked towards the school. "Make sure it stays in your pocket. First impressions count, yeah? You don't want people making fun of you."

Cass shrugged again. "Who cares what they think?" he muttered.

The first bell rang. Suddenly everyone rushed inside Eastbrook Secondary like they were heading to a Stormzy concert and not double Maths.

"Why is everyone so gassed for lessons all of a sudden?" Micah asked, bewildered.

Excited kids sprinted past the two boys. Micah heard snatches of conversation: "big announcement" and "come on, don't want to miss this" and "let's get a decent seat".

What was going on?

The loudspeaker screeched into life. *"Good morning, children. Will all pupils head to the main hall for a very special broadcast? Thank you."*

Micah and Cass shrugged at each other, then followed the kids streaming towards the assembly hall.

This was shaping up to be an interesting morning.

2

Micah and Cass managed to snag the last two seats at the back of the packed assembly hall. The most coveted seats were those in the upper balcony: from those seats up high, you could see everyone else in the hall (and more importantly, stay out of the teachers' sight). But those seats had been taken long ago.

It seemed like everyone at Eastbrook Secondary wanted to catch this special broadcast.

The giant projector screen on stage said:

RICHECORP WORLD BROADCAST
9 A.M. GMT

"Richecorp?" Micah said, puzzled.

"You know Richecorp," Cass said. "They make mobile phone chips. They're, like, the biggest tech company in the world."

"I know who they are," said Micah. "I just don't understand why our school is so hyped about their next product launch."

"Listen, if it means I get to miss PE then I'm not complaining," Cass said. He sat upright, trying to see over the heads of taller students.

Everything is so much bigger compared to primary school, Cass thought: *the stage, the projector screen, the students. Even the toilets.*

Especially the students. Just yesterday, Cass had nearly been crushed by a clumsy Year 11 when he crouched down to get something out of his locker. Back in his old school, Cass was the second tallest in his class.

But here? He was tiny.

A pipsqueak. That's what Micah's friends had called him.

As if Micah could sense his thoughts, he punched Cass lightly on the arm. "Don't take Jamie and Rav's banter too seriously. This is just what secondary school is like," he said.

"It's all right for you. No one's calling you pipsqueak," Cass muttered.

But Micah wasn't listening. He'd taken his battered notebook out of his rucksack and was scribbling away with a stubby pencil. Micah liked to work on his car designs in any spare moment he had.

Cass knew better than to interrupt him when he was in The Zone. Micah's pencil flew furiously over the page. As Cass watched, a supercar materialized on the page.

"Whoa, cool!" Cass said.

"Excuse me! I'll have that, if you don't mind."

A hand came out of nowhere, beckoning for Micah to hand over his notebook. It was Mr Rankford.

"But, sir, assembly hasn't started yet!" Micah protested.

"Drawing pretty pictures is a habit best left behind in primary school, along with play dough and hide and seek," the teacher sneered. "You may collect this at the end of the day."

If there was one thing that scared Cass more than the big kids, it was scary teachers like Mr Rankford. In secondary school, it felt like punishments for breaking a rule were far more severe. And it seemed like there were *hundreds* of these rules.

Micah hunched in his seat. He hoped and prayed that no one else had heard Mr Rankford talk about his "pretty pictures". Jamie and his crew would never let him live it down.

"Don't take it too seriously, bro. This is just

what secondary school is like," Cass smirked.

Micah smiled. "Touché!"

The head teacher took to the stage. "Welcome, students!" Mrs Spencer said. "Today is a very special Friday morning. As you know, one of the world's most innovative companies, Richecorp, is showcasing a major product demo today."

Micah wondered what it could be. Richecorp were known for their super advanced Artificial Intelligence used to power everything from mobile phones to coffee machines. He had never seen or used these products in real life, of course. They were much too expensive for his family.

The coffee machine could make you a hot drink according to how good or bad your day was — a soothing camomile tea after a stressful exam and a frothy hot chocolate to celebrate acing sports day. The mobile phone could sense your mood and help bring you back to normality: if you were tired it would recommend a mood–boosting music playlist, and if you needed cheering up you might find that your phone background wallpaper had changed to a basket of adorable kittens.

Maybe the announcement was about an AI-powered supercar they'd invented?

Micah sat up a little straighter. Now that *would* be something!

"But what you might not know," Mrs Spencer continued, "is that the Founder and CEO of Richecorp started out here at Eastbrook Secondary!"

Murmurs and gasps rippled through the audience. Noel Riche was notoriously private and there was barely a single photograph of him in the public eye. He didn't have Instagram, Twitter or TikTok. His Wikipedia page was full of wild speculation – that he had grown up in the Peruvian jungle, that he could speak fifty-two languages, that he was a genius who had invented his first robot at age four. But it had never occurred to the kids that he might have been a pupil at ordinary old Eastbrook Secondary.

"One of the richest people in the world went to school *here*?" Micah whispered. "No way!"

"I didn't even know he was British!" Cass said.

"That's right!" Mrs Spencer said, beaming with pride at the astonishment in the room. "Noel Riche enrolled at Eastbrook Secondary in 1985."

The image on the projector screen changed. It showed a photo of a gawky school boy with a bad haircut and an oversized blazer. A few chuckles rang through the hall. Whoever this was, he certainly didn't look like a future billionaire.

"What a loser," a girl in the row ahead said to a friend. They giggled quietly.

Cass touched the sleeve of his too-big blazer and felt a tug of recognition. If someone as awkward-looking as Noel Riche could make it through secondary school and become successful, maybe he could too.

"Noel Riche is famous for transforming ordinary objects using Artificial Intelligence," Mrs Spencer went on. "As you all know, Artificial Intelligence is the intelligence displayed by machines. Toasters that can decide how brown you want your toast, fridges that know exactly what to say when you're having a bad day." There was laughter throughout the hall and she held her hand up for silence. "Today, Noel Riche is going to announce the biggest development of his career. I'm sure it will be an inspirational and educational experience for us all." A hush fell over the room. "Noel Riche is proof that, no matter where you are from, you can achieve excellence if you follow your dreams and don't give up."

Yeah, right, Micah thought. How could he follow his dreams when people like Mr Rankford yanked them out of his hands? Or when he was too scared to show anyone his drawings and ideas in case people laughed at him?

Mrs Spencer smiled. "I'll let Noel Riche himself do the talking now. Enjoy."

Suddenly, the projector screen changed again. A countdown clock appeared over an image of a starry night sky.

"The Richecorp world broadcast will begin in two minutes and forty-five seconds," said a computerized voice, booming through the assembly hall speakers.

The students sat up in their chairs, visibly excited and whispering to themselves about what his big announcement could be.

"I bet he's invented something really cool, like Robot Butlers!" someone said.

"I hope he's invented a better haircut," one kid sniggered.

"It's obviously something to do with outer space," Cass said quietly.

The numbers on the timer ticked down to zero. The image of the night sky faded, giving way to a video livestream. A man in a black T-shirt sat behind a huge chrome desk. Richecorp's distinctive circular red logo was stamped on to the front of the desk and on the black T-shirt.

"That's him," breathed Cass.

"Whoa. Noel Riche got an upgrade," Micah said.

It was true. The man was unrecognizable from

the scrawny young boy in the school photo. His iron grey-streaked hair was coiffed in all the right places, and his fashionably understated T-shirt emphasized his muscles. He gave a tight smile and his teeth shone as brightly as the chrome desk.

"Hello. Bonjour. Hola. Konnichiwa," he began. "Right now, this livestream is being beamed across roughly one hundred million devices around the world. As the founder of Richecorp, the number one phone chip provider on the planet, I should know." He flashed that smile again.

"Seems a bit up himself," Micah muttered.

"Shush," Cass whispered. "I want to hear the announcement!"

"I could talk at length about how Richecorp is the most profitable, the fastest-growing and generally the most awesome company in the world, and how this is our most exciting venture yet. But time is money and I don't want to waste either," Mr Riche continued. "So let's cut to the chase, shall we?"

He pressed a button under his desk. The chrome tabletop flipped up to reveal a dashboard of bleeping lights, buttons and dials. It looked *serious*.

Mr Riche tapped a few buttons. The livestream video shrank to the top corner of the screen as footage of the night sky appeared. The camera focused and a blue orb came into view. It was Earth.

"Ooooooh," the audience in the assembly hall said in unison. It was hard not to be impressed.

"Told you," muttered Cass. "Space."

The video became clearer and clearer. What looked like pinpricks of light and weird grey blurs focused into bright stars and hulking meteors suspended in the darkness.

Cass leant forward in his chair. "I've never seen meteors this close before!"

"This guy has cameras in space?" Micah said.

"It looks like he has more than cameras," Cass said.

Amongst the giant grey rocks floated sleek bullet-shaped rockets stamped with Richecorp's logo.

"Why has he sent rockets to look at some floating rocks?" Micah whispered. "Why not go somewhere cool like Mars?"

"What you're looking at is the Noelle Asteroid Belt, named after my dear daughter. At a mere 380,000 km away, it's our nearest celestial neighbour," Mr Riche said. "I'm proud to say it's the first ever artificially-created asteroid belt. Every single one of those asteroids was placed there, deliberately, by myself."

Cass froze. Cass's astronomy brain whirred into gear; he knew that having giant asteroids just 380,000 km away was dangerously close. That was even closer than the moon! What if they spun out of orbit and made contact with Earth?

Why is Noel Riche so chill? Cass wondered.

"My latest invention is nearly forty years in the making. It is no understatement to say that it will change the world as we know it." Mr Riche leaned back on his chair and lifted both legs so that his feet were resting on the chrome desk.

It was the sort of thing that would definitely get you in trouble at school, Micah thought, but maybe the rules were different for billionaires.

"Let me begin with a story. Back when I was a young boy with a dream at my dump of a secondary school, Eastbrook Secondary."

The audience gasped. Mrs Spencer turned bright red. This was clearly not how she had expected the broadcast to go. There were a few nervous titters.

"I was a smart kid, as you might guess," said Noel Riche. "Aced science and maths. One day in Year 7, I designed something that I thought was truly revolutionary. A prototype for a space rocket that can hit a target on earth with 99.9% accuracy! I was so proud when I presented it to the class. But do you think anyone cared?" Noel Riche laughed bitterly. "Of course not. No one understood my vision. My genius. Some of the kids even laughed. They threw stones at me! The teacher told me to stop letting my imagination run away with me and focus on the textbook in front of me."

Cass felt a bit sorry for Mr Riche. All those years later and he was still upset about being teased.

"That sounds rough," he whispered to Micah, who nodded.

"But they won't be laughing now," Noel Riche said in a quiet voice. "You see, these rockets you can see on screen — they aren't ordinary rockets. They're missiles. And they are aimed straight at Earth."

Cass gasped. "Bro, I don't like the sound of this…"

Mr Riche smiled a shark-tooth grin. "If you're a viewer in London, in the United Kingdom, then I urge you to look to the skies. Particularly students at Eastbrook Secondary. You won't want to miss this," he snarled.

3

The students of Eastbrook Secondary didn't need to be told twice. Hundreds of them stampeded to their nearest window while the teachers tried (and failed) to maintain control.

Luckily for Micah and Cass, they were sat close to the nearest window. Micah jumped towards the glass – he wasn't going to miss this.

"Micah, this doesn't feel right," Cass shouted over the chaos. His instinct was to find somewhere safe and hide, not clamber to

the nearest window. Something was very, very wrong about this whole thing.

"Everyone back to their seats!" shouted the teachers, but the kids ignored them. They all stared transfixed out of the window, eyes to the sky.

"Look! Can you see it?" one kid shouted.

"What are you talking about? That's a helicopter," another replied.

"No, they're shooting stars!" Micah yelled.

It was unmistakable. The grey October sky was filled with beautiful streaks of bright light peeking through the clouds, like a daytime firework display. The kids *oohed* and *aahed* as the glowing yellow streaks turned a vibrant orange.

"It's a meteor shower," Cass said under his breath.

"You call that a meteor?" one kid sniffed. "I've eaten pizzas bigger than that!"

"Don't underestimate it just because it's small," murmured Cass. His eyes were fixed uneasily on the rocks streaking towards them. Everyone else seemed thrilled.

"This is so cool!"

"Science in action!"

But their delight was short-lived. One of the orange streaks hurtled towards them. In a matter of seconds, the streak became visible as a grey rock the size of a football tumbling through the sky.

BOOM!

The meteor crashed into the staff car park, exploding into a giant fireball that soared twelve feet into the air.

"NO! My car!" Mr Rankford screamed. "How am I going to explain this to the insurers?!"

The students screamed and gasped. Of all the things they expected to see on a Friday morning, Mr Rankford's Volvo being destroyed by a meteorite was not one of them.

Another asteroid whistled through the air and, *SMASH*, the netball court was a smoking ruin.

Another struck the bike rack, pulverizing steel and rubber into a cloud of flame and smoke.

Another took out the bins.

A voice piped up from the assembly hall speakers and the kids swung back to look at the screen. Unbelievably, Noel Riche's broadcast was still being live-streamed.

"For those of you who don't know much about meteorites or space rocks, let me enlighten you," he said. "Most meteorites burn up or crumble when they enter the Earth's atmosphere and therefore cause very little damage." He gave that toothy grin again. *"My* meteorites, however, are no ordinary grey rocks. They're specially designed to withstand re-entry into the earth's atmosphere without crumbling. Paired with Richecorp's laser-precision rocket launchers, they make quite the team. They can cause a *lot* of damage – as I think the students at Eastbrook Secondary have just found out."

"He targeted us on purpose!" Cass exlcaimed.

"What is this dude's problem?" Micah said.

Noel Riche stood from behind his chrome desk and smoothed his T-shirt. "Rest assured, this is just the beginning. A light sprinkling, if you will. Just a little taster. It can end here – if, that is, the world governments hand over power to me."

Everyone in the assembly hall, students and teachers alike, faced the projector screen. The only sound piercing the tense silence was Mr Rankford hyperventilating into a paper bag.

"Now, so far the meteorites I've deployed are tiny little things, like marbles compared to a cannon ball. Currently orbiting Earth are six giant meteorites, waiting for me to press the button and deploy them from the safety of my bomb-proof bunker. Just one of these asteroids could devastate a continent. Several of these asteroids could destroy life on Earth as we know it," Noel Riche scowled. "Do not attempt to negotiate with me. World leaders, you have one hour to hand over power to me. And I mean all of it. Executive power, your militaries, your navies, your air forces, the lot. One hour. I won't wait one second more."

The livestream disappeared. A countdown

timer appeared in its place and started counting down from sixty minutes.

"One hour!" cried Micah.

"It's starting now!" Cass said. "Look. Fifty-nine minutes. And counting!"

Suddenly, both Micah and Cass's phones vibrated in their blazer pockets. There was no need to hide their phones from the teachers: they were far too concerned trying to calm the frantic students racing towards the exit.

"Right! Form two orderly lines this instant," Mrs Spencer yelled. Somehow her voice cut through the pandemonium and soon the students made two sort-of neat queues leading to the assembly hall exits.

Micah unlocked his phone. Along with several missed calls from Mum and panicked text messages from Dad, he saw a message from someone new.

Meet me outside the school car park.

NOW. No time to waste.

The number was unknown.

"Hey, Cass," Micah said, "did you get this weird message too?" He looked up. "Cass?"

His little brother was nowhere to be seen. Students rushed towards the hall doors, cramming the narrow exit with a sea of bodies.

Micah swallowed. If Cass got caught in a stampede, Mum would ground him for life. She had made it *very* clear that looking after him at school was Micah's responsibility.

"Bro, I'm down here!" Cass yelled. He was hunched in a corner of the hall. "If another meteorite hits, this is the safest place to be."

"Cass, we need to get out," Micah said. "I got this weird text – someone wants to meet us outside."

"Ignore it! It's a trap! Likely a mass text sent

by Noel Riche. He probably wants us all outside so he can finish the job," Cass shrieked, his eyes wide with terror.

Micah crouched down beside him. "Listen, bro. I know you're scared, but we need to get out of here sooner or later," he said. "And you never know, maybe whoever sent this text can help us?"

Micah couldn't explain it, but he had a feeling that this text message was the real deal. That they should go and meet whoever had sent it.

Cass nodded. He crawled out of his hiding spot and dusted off his blazer. The doors were still crammed with students fighting their way out.

"C'mon," Micah said. "I know another route."

Cass followed his brother to the back of the hall where they climbed upstairs to the balcony level. Micah went to the very back and carefully felt along the wood-panelled walls. He pressed against one raised bit of wood. With a click, the panel swung open revealing a space behind it.

"Whoa. A trap door!" Cass said, impressed.

Micah chuckled. "Not quite. This is the projector room. I helped out last month on the tech side when we did our first Year 7 assembly."

They stood in a dimly lit room stuffed with boxes while Micah fumbled for the light switch. The room was flooded with harsh fluorescent light.

"Call Mum and Dad. We can hide here until they're ready to pick us up. I've got supplies for the both of us! Well, a ham sandwich," Cass said.

"No," said Micah firmly. "I want to find out who sent that text. We need to get outside." He clambered over a pile of boxes.

Finally, Micah found what he was looking for: a fire exit door leading to a stairwell hidden from students. It led straight to the staff car park.

"Attention all students," Mrs Spencer said over the tannoy. *"Please head to the canteen at once.*

Do not, and I repeat, do not attempt to leave school grounds."

"Won't we get in trouble for leaving?" Cass asked.

"Bro, Mr Rankford's car got vaporized before our eyes! Whatever's going on now is a much bigger deal than detention."

The boys pushed open the fire door and ran down the stairs. Within minutes they had left the school.

They had made it outside.

Micah jogged around the side of the school, closely followed by Cass.

"Watch out for the teachers!" Micah said. They both put their backs against a nearby wall and kept close to it as they made their way to the car park.

But the teachers were too busy calming down frantic parents and guardians, who had already gathered outside the school gate. They were being let into the school in small groups so they could collect their kids and race home before Noel Riche unleashed chaos.

Cass checked the time on his phone. "Thirty-eight minutes to go."

Micah wasn't listening. He was too busy scanning the car park for whoever had texted him.

But there was no one.

He couldn't help but feel disappointed.

"I told you that text message wasn't worth paying attention to," Cass said. "There's no one here."

Suddenly, a *vroom* sound could be heard in the distance. Micah and Cass felt a wind whip around them, knocking their school ties into their faces. But where was it coming from?

"You feel that, bro?" Micah said. "The wind's not coming from the sky!"

"Ahhh!" the boys screamed.

It appeared so quickly it may as well have been conjured by magic. A ramshackle maroon car appeared seemingly out of thin air. It zoomed closer, making an awful screeching sound, and Micah noticed that it boasted a hasty paint job that didn't quite cover the rust. Even worse, the rear windscreen was cracked and the bumper scraped along the ground.

"What scrap heap did this car crawl out of?" he asked. "It looks like it's several different makes and models combined."

"It's going quite fast, though, isn't it?" said Cass. "For such an old banger."

"Yeah," said Micah thoughtfully. "It is."

The car jerked to a halt beside them and the back passenger door (which was silver, Micah noticed) swung open.

"Get in! There's no time to lose," came a voice from inside.

The voice sounded like it came from an

elderly man – quavery and faint. The tinted windows meant that neither of them could see the driver. They knew better than to get into a strange car.

"Give us one good reason why!" Micah yelled.

"I can give you two!" the man said. "And they'll be here in three … two…"

The wind whipped the air into a frenzy again.

A new vrooming sound filled the air – the sound of another engine. But this wasn't any engine Micah recognized. His finely tuned ear could tell the difference between a Lexus and a Lamborghini by sound alone. This engine growled like a big cat. Like the tigers he saw at the zoo.

Suddenly, as though also conjured by magic, another car popped into view. This one was entirely different to the maroon monstrosity. Again, it was an unidentified make – Micah couldn't name it at all – and it was made of shimmery silver so highly polished it reflected the outside world like a mirror.

"Whoa," Micah said under his breath. "Now that is something."

It was like no car he'd ever seen before. The supercar looked like it had rolled out of the twenty-second century, or the set of a sci-fi movie. Even the way the engine purred was music to Micah's ears.

He slowly stepped towards it, arms outreached.

"Oi," hissed Cass. "What are you doing? This is the car that the person in the old banger warned us about!"

"I just want to touch it!" Micah murmured, still walking forward as if in a trance.

"I'm warning you," croaked the old man's voice from the battered car, *"get in the car now if you value your life."*

The doors of the supercar swung open. A young girl with a slick dark-brown ponytail leaped out of the passenger seat. Even though she looked about Micah's age, she had the air of someone who had left childhood behind long ago. Her navy tracksuit was so sharp it had right angles, and not a single strand of hair was out of place. Although the brothers had definitely never seen her before, she looked vaguely familiar.

Her eyes landed on Micah and Cass. She broke into a cold smile. "You are making this entirely too easy," she said haughtily.

"What do you want?" Micah asked.

Cass inched towards the ramshackle car. "Micah, I think we should make a move!"

"Grunton!" yelled the girl. "The targets are trying to escape."

A huge man slid out of the supercar's driver's seat. He was dressed in black with a peaked chauffeur's cap and reflective sunglasses. Grunton was so big and broad he seemed to blot out the sunlight just by standing up. He flipped open an extendable baton and lumbered towards the boys, the sun bouncing off the polished buttons on his black suit.

"Micah and Cass, get in this instant!" yelled the man from the maroon car.

Cass grabbed Micah's arm and shook him. His brother blinked, took in the giant with the baton, and ran.

The rear passenger-side door was still open. They threw themselves into the seat. The door slammed itself shut and the ramshackle car sped off.

4

The car zoomed through the streets of their neighbourhood at dizzying speeds. But with the silver car on their tail, Micah and Cass couldn't exactly enjoy the chase.

"Let's get you strapped in. Safety first, fellas!" a voice said.

Suddenly, thick seat belts launched out of the chair and strapped both boys into their seats.

Micah blinked. That was super-advanced — as was the speed that they were travelling at. It didn't make any sense. How come this supercar looked like it was made from garbage?

The car's interior was as ill-matched as its exterior. The seats were stitched together from brown leather, grey cloth and something metallic that looked and felt just like tin foil. Yet the two seats in front had touchscreens in the back of the headrest – Micah knew that those didn't come cheap.

"Er, how about you tell us your name since you know ours?" Cass said, addressing the driver's seat. He lunged forward and peered round. "Aaaaaaaah!" he screamed.

"What?" snapped Micah. "Don't do that, you'll scare the driver."

"Micah, it's a driverless car!" Cass said, eyes wide with wonder.

Micah peered round at the front seats. Cass was right. There was no one driving the car.

"But we heard that voice!" whimpered Cass.

"Who was talking?"

Micah thought fast. "The person talking isn't real. It must be AI!"

He shook his head. Artificial Intelligence this advanced? No way. That sort of technology only existed in Silicon Valley laboratories. And yet, here they were, being driven by a driverless car at terrifying speed through the streets of their neighbourhood, with a silver bullet in pursuit.

"Who are you? How do you know our names?" Micah shouted.

The car chose not to answer, just shot round a corner at lightning speed. Their neighbourhood soon turned into a blur as they dashed through side streets and alleyways. But the supercar stayed close, as though drawn to them by an invisible magnet.

"Excuse me," said Cass, trying to sound polite. "I know you're very busy right now, but could you possibly tell us your name?"

"My official name is MK-893000," the voice said through the speaker. *"But my inventors decided to call me Frankenstein for a laugh on account of my appearance. You might have noticed that I'm composed of many different parts, just like Frankenstein's monster. You may call me Frank."*

"Who's chasing us? And why did that big guy look like he wanted to turn us into burger meat?" Micah demanded.

"Steady on, Young Micah! I've got all the answers right here. Just give me two ticks. I'm not very good at the ol' multi-tasking," Frank said. *"And they're gaining on us."*

SMASH!

There was an almighty crash from behind, forcing the boys to lunge forward in their seats. They turned and looked through the smashed rear window.

The supercar was just inches away.

"I hope you have a plan, Frank, 'cause we're

about to be pulverized!" Micah yelled.

"I'm on it!" Frank replied.

The car took a sharp right turn into a narrow side street. Micah and Cass peeked through the rear window and saw the silver supercar screech to a halt. The side street was too narrow for the beast of a car to squeeze through.

"Good work, Frank!" Cass said.

Micah looked outside again as the maroon car's bumper spun away and rolled down the road. The car was falling apart – and they were stuck inside, travelling at breakneck speed.

He tugged at the seatbelt, but it wouldn't budge.

"We're stuffed," he whispered to Cass.

"Phew! Now that we've lost them, I can show you the movie. Sit back, relax and enjoy," Frank said.

"Relax!" yelled Micah. "Is he serious?"

"Shh," Cass whispered back. "Let's see what information Frank has for us."

The headrest screens flickered to life. Two men dressed in metallic jumpsuits appeared on the screen. One of them clutched a wrench so hard his knuckles had turned from light brown to white.

"They look kinda familiar," Cass said.

"Um, hi boys!" said the taller man. "If you're watching this then you already know we're in serious trouble."

"There's no easy way to say this," said the shorter man, "but the future of the world is in your hands."

"I know what you're thinking. Micah, I bet you're wondering if there are hidden cameras somewhere?" asked the tall man.

"And Cass, you're probably calculating the probability of how you can escape this car without breaking a bone," said the shorter man.

Cass gasped. "How did he know that?!"

"The reason we know this is because we're, well, you. Just twenty-two years older. I'm Future Micah," the taller man said.

"And I'm Future Cass," the shorter guy said.

Cass crossed his arms. "This sucks! Can't believe I'm shorter than you in the future too."

"Listen carefully because we have a very important mission for you," Future Cass continued. "We need you to stop Noel Riche before he takes over the world."

"A bit too late for that! He's already threatened to destroy every continent!" Micah yelled at the screen.

"The thing is, Noel wasn't always a supervillain with an arsenal of space rockets at his disposal," Future Micah said. "We found out that he was actually a sweet kid. But then he got bullied badly at school and something changed."

"They threw stones at him," Cass said quietly, recalling what Noel Riche had said earlier.

"Right, so it's clear something went wrong with young Noel. We've been tracking him carefully through time and we think it began one assembly in 1985 at Eastbrook Secondary," said Future Cass. "This is where you boys come in. We need you to step in and prevent this moment from ever happening. I did the calculations and this is our best chance of success."

The two men looked at each other. "In fact, it's our *only* chance of success," Future Micah said.

"If you fail, Noel Riche will run the world of the future with an iron fist. Ninety-nine per cent of the global population works for him in terrible conditions, including us. Believe me, boys, it ain't pretty," Future Cass grimaced.

"But Young Noel Riche wasn't a lost cause. There was still good in him. You need to meet Young Noel, go to school with him, try to make friends with him and set him on a better path," Future Micah said. "Persuade him to use his powers for good rather than evil."

Cass gave a nervous laugh. "But to do that, we'd have to…"

Future Cass nodded. "That's right. We need you to travel back to 1985. Old Frank might not look like much, but he's a very sophisticated time travel machine. I should know, I calibrated him myself."

Micah and Cass looked at each other. They weren't expecting *this*.

Micah said, "You … want us to go back in time … in a time machine?"

"That's right. When you get there, find

Poppa. You can use his boxing gym as the base of operations. Tell him your mission and he'll help you," Future Micah said.

"Now, there's a high chance Poppa will think you're making this all up. He won't know who you are. That's why we left his Olympic gold medal in the glove compartment – along with a few other vital items," Future Cass said. "We've given you all you need to fulfil your quest – we hope."

"The medal will prove to him that you're definitely family. If he still doesn't believe you, introduce him to Frank. If a talking car doesn't persuade him you're from the future, I don't know what will," Future Micah said. "Or you could always tell him about the family birth mark... You know, the one on our left bum—"

"They know about the birthmark, bro!" Future Cass interrupted. He turned back to the camera. "We need to warn you about someone.

Watch out for Noel Riche's daughter, Noelle. She's the heir to his global empire, and she will do whatever it takes to make sure *nothing* threatens her inheritance. Even if it means following you through time and space. Noel Riche will make sure she and her chauffeur-bodyguard are armed to the teeth."

"Richecorp's spy drones are all over the city. That's why we're hiding in this underground bunker. It's likely they've uncovered our plans and sent Noelle to thwart them," Future Micah said.

Cass turned to his brother. "That was the creepy angry girl!"

"But don't worry, I'm pretty sure we lost them before the wormhole was activated," Future Micah said.

"But just in case," Future Cass said, "look out for a silver car that's far more advanced than anything you've ever seen. I have a feeling that car won't blend in so easily. Steer well clear, OK? She may look young, but her mission is to stop you by any means necessary."

Micah swallowed anxiously.

"One more thing! Anything you do in the past can affect the future in ways we can't even imagine," said Future Micah seriously. "That means you have to be incredibly careful not to change anything, or you might do more harm than good. Don't tell anyone why you're there except for Poppa. Stick to essential information about the mission."

"Is this really happening, bro?" Cass said, feeling awed.

The lights flickered in the background of the video. "We only have a few seconds of power left!" Future Micah said.

The video cut out. The screens went black.

The car turned a tight corner and slammed Micah and Cass against each other. They looked out of the window: the silver supercar had caught up with them again.

"Ouch! Frank, you have human passengers, remember?" Micah yelled.

"Sorry, kiddo. I need to pick up speed if I'm gonna make it to the wormhole and activate the time travel protocol!"

"Wormhole?!" Micah yelled. "What's a wormhole?"

"Future-you mentioned it, bro – they're special portals that allow travel through time and space!" Cass yelled.

"Do you believe this, Cass? It sounds like something from a sci-fi movie!" Micah said.

"Theoretically, time travel is possi-WHOA!" Cass jolted forward as Frank picked up speed.

"It's now or never, lads. Should I activate the temporal wormhole using the programmed coordinates?" Frank asked.

Suddenly, the supercar rammed into Frank

with such force that the boys felt like marbles in a tin can. The car fishtailed wildly, hit the curb and flipped.

The boys looked at each other. "Activate it!" they screamed.

The last thing Cass saw before he shielded his face was an upside-down shop window.

For a split-second they felt weightless. The boys heard a loud POP, they smelled hot coffee, their teeth vibrated and time seemed to stop completely.

Then everything went dark.

5

A millennium or a millisecond later – *who knew?* – Micah opened his eyes. Everything was perfectly still.

He turned to the figure slumped next to him. "Bro, are you all right?"

Cass didn't move for a second, then shot upright, eyes wild with panic. "I had the wildest dream! A terrifying supervillain was about to destroy Earth and we had to go back in time to stop him!"

"Welcome to 1985, boys. The wormhole …

transition … is … complete," Frank said, wheezing as though he was out of breath.

"Wait!" said Cass, blinking. "That wasn't a dream? There really is a terrifying villain about to destroy Earth and we've gone back in time to stop him?"

"I'm afraid so. Frank, where are we?" Micah asked.

"*When* are we would be the better question," Cass said.

A clunking sound came from the engine, followed by a groan. Frank didn't sound too great.

"Local time … 11:22 hours. Local date … 1st May, 1985," Frank rasped.

Cass's eyes widened with disbelief. "We've gone back in time to before we were even born."

Frank let out another groaning wheeze.

"Hey, Frank, are you all right? I can take a

look at the engine if you want," Micah said. He didn't know much about time travelling cars compared to normal ones, but he could give it a shot.

"I've survived worse," Frank chuckled. *"Just sustained a fair bit of damage in the chase. The good news is that we lost Noelle and her supercar during the wormhole transition … I think."*

"You *think*?" Micah said. "Thanks for the reassurance."

"What do you think Noelle wants with us?" Cass asked.

"You heard our future selves in that video. Her mission is to eliminate us," Micah said soberly. "So we have to keep our heads down."

"Why don't you lads get out?" said Frank. *"Stretch your legs. Check out the past."*

The car doors creaked open and Micah and Cass climbed out. The car was perched on top of a tower block car park, five storeys high. From the top of the building, East London sprawled out beneath them, but it wasn't a skyline that the brothers recognized.

"No Olympic Park, no Westfield Shopping Centre… We really have gone back several decades," Micah said.

"Boys? Don't forget this," Frank said. "Your proof for your grandpa."

The glovebox flipped open.

"Oh yeah! Our future selves said they left us supplies for our mission too," Cass said. "I bet they left us some *sick* gadgets!"

Micah climbed into the driver's seat and rooted around in the glovebox. "It's an envelope," he said, sounding disappointed.

"It's obviously a trick to put off thieves, Micah!" Cass said, climbing into the passenger seat. "Have you never seen a spy movie before? Open it!"

Micah dumped the contents of the beige

envelope out on to the dashboard. They stared at the little pile in silence.

Their future selves had left them nothing but … junk.

"I don't believe it," Micah said. "What are we supposed to do with *this*? It looks like they emptied out Mum's handbag!"

"There must be a reason for it," Cass said. "Our future selves invented a time-travelling car! It might look like rubbish, but you never know."

Micah began to sort through the pile, holding each item up one by one. "Cass, here is what they left us: Poppa's Olympic gold medal, an arcade ticket with the letters GC on it, a ten pence coin, an old receipt, a crumpled fiver, a safety pin and a rusty key."

"There's got to be more," Cass said. He took the envelope and shook it. Something rattled.

His eyes lit up. "See, I told you!" He fished out two metal pins that glinted in the late morning sunlight.

Micah took a closer look. "They're just school pins! See that? It's the Eastbrook Secondary school crest."

"Nah," said Cass. "There must be more to them."

"Young Cass has a point," Frank interrupted. *"Those pins are walkie-talkies in disguise. Pop them on your blazers and we can stay in contact within a three-mile radius. Perfect for undercover work — for when you infiltrate the school."*

"So we're saving the future of the planet with a handful of rubbish and dusty radios? Why did they send us back here without any proper gear?" Micah sulked.

"Because if two boys roamed the streets of 1985 with stun guns and hoverboards, it would make headline news! And that could jeopardize the future in a million different ways," Frank said sternly. *"You need to keep a low profile. Your mission is to make friends with young Noel Riche and help him find a better way. And you don't need futuristic gadgets to do that."*

"Fine," said Micah with a sigh. "Let's go to the school and find Noel."

"Our future selves told us to find Poppa first," Cass reminded him.

"Fine. It's better than sitting on top of this roof in the boiling sun all day," Micah said, taking off his school tie. Just a few moments ago, they were in October. "I'm not dressed for summer."

"Hey, Frank, how do we find Poppa's boxing gym?" Cass asked.

"Can't help you there, sonny. My GPS doesn't work in 1985."

"Of course!" Cass muttered. "GPS isn't widely used yet."

Micah squinted at Cass. "How come you remember useless information like that but can't find your own way to school?"

"I'm afraid you'll have to find the boxing gym the old-fashioned way," Frank said.

Micah and Cass looked at each other, puzzled. "How?" they asked at the same time.

Frank chuckled. *"Try asking for directions! Now, if you'll excuse me, I need a nap. My battery life ain't what it used to be."*

The car made a sound like yawning, followed by some heavy clunking in the engine. The headlights clicked off and the car was still.

"Frank? Fraaaaank? Can you just give us a hint?" Micah asked.

A robotic voice piped up from the car speaker.

"Damage detected to navigation systems. Repair procedure in operation."

"It's no use, Micah. We need to find Poppa ourselves," Cass said.

"Yeah," said Micah. "The old-fashioned way – whatever that means."

When Micah and Cass had reached the ground floor of the car park, they followed traffic sounds to Stratford High Street. It didn't take them long to realize that Frank hadn't taken them very far. They were in their usual neighbourhood – but it didn't look the same at all.

"Hey, Micah! I swear that laundrette is where the fancy bakery used to be. I mean, where the fancy bakery *will* be in the future," Cass said. "Time travel is confusing."

"Check the street signs – we're only a few minutes from home," Micah said.

"Do you think we could see the house?" Cass

said excitedly. "Maybe Mum or Dad will be close by!"

Micah shook his head. "They definitely won't be, bro. Mum and Dad weren't born until 1987."

"So we're really alone, huh?" Cass said rather quietly.

Micah put one hand on his brother's shoulder. "Just until we find Poppa."

They walked down the quiet high street looking for any sign of a boxing gym. Apart from some weird haircuts and cars booming the same ancient pop songs their dad sang in the shower, they didn't see anything at all. The modern coffee shop chains and high street stores they were used to were now grocers, music record shops and a greasy spoon diner – but no boxing gym.

"If our phones worked, we could find the boxing gym in two minutes," Micah grumbled.

"Bro, look!" Cass said, pointing across the

street to a grand old building with wide steps and ornate pillars. "Game City. It's an arcade. GC. Doesn't the logo look familiar?"

"Now isn't the time for video games," Micah muttered. "We're on a mission."

Cass rooted through the envelope and pulled out a piece of paper. "See, the arcade ticket they left us is for this place." The letters GC were framed in a circle.

"I'm not convinced anything in that envelope is useful," Micah sniffed.

"It's got to mean something," Cass said.

Micah paused. "You hear that?"

A very faint growling sound in the distance. Like a mechanical tiger.

"It's just traffic," Cass said, but he felt uneasy.

"We need to hide!" Micah said, pulling his brother into a nearby alley in the nick of time.

A few seconds later, the silver supercar drove by. The boys stayed in the shadows as it pulled to a stop. They heard a door open and slam, followed by footsteps.

Micah slowly, carefully, peeked out. He saw Noelle approach a newspaper vendor on the street corner.

"What can you see, bro?" Cass asked, his back pressed against a cold brick wall.

"She's talking to people around the neighbourhood," he said. They were close enough to hear traces of their conversation.

"Have you seen two young boys in school uniform, one short and one tall?" Noelle asked.

Micah ducked back into the alleyway.

"So Noelle made it through the wormhole," whispered Micah. "Great. Now we've got her on our tail – just in case this mission wasn't impossible enough."

"How did you know they were close?"

"I would know the sound of that engine a mile off," Micah said. "I've never heard anything like it before. Doesn't it remind you of a wild animal?"

Cass shrugged. "All engines sound the same to me, bro."

When Micah was sure the supercar had driven away, he and his brother crept out of the shadows and back into the bright sunshine. "That was too close," he said. "It's not safe for us to roam the streets. We need to know where we're going."

"Exactly. So let's go to the arcade and ask someone for directions," Cass said. "And maybe we'll also find out why we've got this ticket."

Micah nodded. "Fine. Let's do it."

6

Micah and Cass walked up to the entrance of Game City and pushed through the heavy tinted doors. Inside, it didn't look quite as impressive. The dark red carpet was threadbare and the whole building smelled of stale popcorn and old socks. A few older teenagers were clustered round the various machines, whooping and laughing as they battled it out on the massive, clunky machines.

"This is where people went for *fun*?" Micah said. So far, 1985 was making him feel very grateful for the 2020s and very sorry for his parents. "I guess they didn't have many options."

Cass, though, couldn't have been happier. A whole building dedicated to his favourite old-school games? And no one around to tease him for it? He practically wanted to move in. He would get used to the funky smell.

"This," he whispered, his eyes shining, "is amazing. And there are no queues 'cause everyone is at school!"

Without waiting for Micah, Cass slid his ticket into a slot that unlocked a revolving metal gate and pushed through. The gate clicked behind him.

"Um, bro? How do I get in without a ticket?" Micah asked.

But Cass had disappeared, lured by the bright lights of a pinball machine.

"Oi, Cass!" Micah yelled. "Come back!"

"Take a chill pill, little man," said a voice. A

teenage boy winked at Micah before giving the metal gate a hard shove with his hip. The gate clicked open and Micah hurried through.

"Thanks, mate," Micah said, feeling a bit silly.

He jogged around the arcade until he found Cass gazing up in awe at a bright yellow video game. The sign at the top read Pac-Man in bright neon letters.

"Um," said Micah, "we're in the middle of a mission, you know, and it's kinda urgent."

Cass shook his head slowly, his eyes still fixed on the

gleaming machine. "Bro, you don't understand. This is, like, the holy grail of 1980s video games. These machines are worth thousands of pounds in the future. But here it's only ten pence to play!"

"The game can wait. We need to find someone who can tell us where the boxing gym is," Micah said. "To find Poppa, remember?"

"Hold on," Cass said. "If our future selves wanted us to ask someone for directions, we could have done that at any shop in the high street. But they wanted us here. In the arcade. Why is that?"

"Because Future Cass is even more obsessed with dumb games than you?" Micah said.

"Nah, that's not it. Remember they know us better than we know ourselves. There's a clue here waiting for us. We just need to do what future us expect us to do."

Micah sighed and looked around. "OK,

genius. What would future us expect us to do in an arcade?"

Cass smiled and tapped the machine beside him. "Play Pac-Man!"

Before his brother could stop him, Cass slipped the ten pence coin from the envelope into the slot.

The screen lit up and the game began.

Although Micah couldn't see the appeal of these old-school video games, he had to admit: Cass had skills. He played the game like he was born to do it, navigating the little round yellow face as it consumed the dots on the screen.

Cass was in gaming heaven. He rattled through level after level, his wrist rotating the joystick with ease. It was just like the retro gaming console he had at home. Suddenly, finding Poppa didn't seem so urgent. He was in the zone, just like when Micah was designing a new car in his sketchbook.

Suddenly, the machine bleeped even louder than usual. "*New top score!*" It announced.

"I'm a champ! I'm a champ!" yelled Cass.

"Keep your voice down, bro! Remember we're being pursued," Micah whispered.

"All right! Let me soak up my victory," Cass grinned. "Besides, I can't leave without putting my initials in the scoreboard."

Micah glanced around uneasily. "OK. Make it quick!"

This turned out to be impossible. The silly game didn't have anything as useful as a keyboard. Instead, Cass had to painstakingly rotate with the joystick through the entire alphabet in order to find his initials "CGB".

Suddenly, the heavy doors of Game City slammed shut. The noise reverberated around the quiet of the mostly empty arcade.

"Cass, we've wasted enough time here already." Micah tugged his brother's arm. "Seriously, the last thing we need is more trouble. Let's go."

"That's weird," said Cass, frowning at the screen. "The game scoreboard has put my initials twice. I definitely didn't play two games."

"What does it matter? Maybe the second top-scorer has the same initials as you!" Micah said.

"And exactly the same top score?" Cass's eyes went wide. "You're right! Who else has the same initials as me…? Me! The other player is Future Cass. *This is our clue!*"

The boys looked around but there was nothing but old carpet and crumbs.

Micah got down on his knees and checked around the gaming machine. He saw a flash of white in the gap between the yellow machine and the wall. Something rectangular was stuck there with tape. He stretched out his hand…

"Hurry up, bro!" Cass said, backing away from the machine.

"Nearly … got it," Micah huffed. The tips of his fingers touched the rectangular object and he began to peel back the tape.

Finally, Micah ripped off the small white parcel and tugged it out.

Suddenly, Cass slammed himself against the wall and crouched down next to his brother. "Shhh!" he said, putting a finger to his mouth.

"I'm sure they aren't foolish enough to be playing games at a time like this, but we must leave no stone unturned, Grunton."

"As you wish, Miss Noelle," a gravelly voice replied.

Micah and Cass froze. Their pursuers were so close.

Noelle and Grunton checked each part of the arcade methodically. If Micah and Cass didn't come up with a plan fast, it was only a matter of time before they were found.

They heard Noelle's voice become a bit louder. She was getting closer. "When we eventually stop these low lifes from carrying out their plan, I want everyone to know it was thanks to me," Noelle said. "After this, Father will see me as more than worthy of leading the Richecorp empire."

"It is a role you have been raised for from birth," Grunton said.

"True. But I cannot take any chances. Father must know that I am up to the task."

Micah gulped. There was something about the steeliness in her voice that made him believe she was more than capable of doing whatever it took to stop them.

"Aha!" Noelle said. "We must check the bathrooms. Grunton, if you see them hiding, do not harm them. I would like to do that myself," she snarled.

"As you wish, Miss Noelle," Grunton said.

The boys heard the bathroom doors slam. This was their chance.

"Move move move!" Micah whispered.

The two boys got up, raced through the arcade and hopped over the dodgy entrance gate. They didn't stop running until the arcade was well behind them.

They ducked into a side street and slowed down to catch their breath.

"Bro, did you hear her?" Micah said. "We have to steer well clear of that girl. She means business."

Cass sighed with relief. "That was a close one! But we nailed it: I got the high score and you found the clue."

Micah took a closer look at the clue. It wasn't a package after all but a small book. Except it didn't just have words inside. It had maps. Page after page of them.

"It's called *London A–Z*," Micah said, flicking through the book. "And there's a page folded down."

He flicked to the page and a smile crept across his face. There, on a corner of the page, was a point on the map circled in red.

"Looks like we've found Poppa," Micah grinned.

7

Armed with the confidence of tracking down their first clue, Micah and Cass used the map to find Poppa's boxing gym. But they had one problem: neither of them had ever used a paper map before.

"I'm telling you, bro, we've been walking in the wrong direction for ages," Cass muttered. "We were meant to take a left on to Bedale Street. Do you see the sign for Bedale Street anywhere?"

Micah thrust the London A–Z into Cass's hands. "You navigate, then!"

But Cass didn't fare much better. His natural aptitude for solving mathematical equations didn't exactly help him here. He was too used to using the map on his phone with the little blue dot showing his exact location.

Cass rotated the map in his hands as if a new angle would make it easier to read. "Why is the text so small? This is impossible!"

Micah smirked. "Not as easy as it looks, is it?"

They soon found their way back to the high street, not far from where they'd started.

"We've been walking in circles!" Cass said.

A familiar shop sign caught Micah's eye. "Hey, bro. Are you seeing what I'm seeing?" he asked, pointing across the road.

Cass looked up. "Khan's Off Licence," he read aloud. "Wow! They've been there for nearly forty years."

"Let's go in and ask for directions," Micah said.

They walked into the corner shop. Apart from a fresh lick of white paint on the walls, it looked much the same as they remembered.

"Good afternoon, boys. Can I help you?" a familiar voice asked.

Micah and Cass couldn't believe their eyes. It was Mrs Khan, except she was way younger, with long black hair and no reading glasses perched on her nose. She still had the same warm voice and kind smile.

"Um ... yeah, we're looking for Champion's Boxing Gym. Do you know it?" Micah asked.

Mrs Khan laughed. "Know it? It is practically my husband's second home," she said before giving them directions.

"That was so weird," Cass muttered as they left the shop. "I wonder who else we will meet here that we already know."

"Whatever we do, we can't let them know anything about the future. Remember what our future selves said? It could have serious consequences if we do."

As they walked towards the boxing gym, the brothers discussed what to tell Poppa.

"We just tell him the truth," Micah said at last. "There's nothing else we can do. After all, we've got his Olympic medal as proof."

At last, they reached a sign that said Champion's Boxing Gym. The sign was fixed to a multi-storey building on the street corner with other businesses on either side – it sort of looked like a warehouse from the outside.

"Look, Micah! The boxing gym is only down the road from our school. How come we've never seen it?" Cass asked.

Micah shrugged. "Weird, right? Dad drives me to the boxing ring across town. This one probably doesn't exist in our time. Must have been torn down to make way for flats or something."

"What do you think he's like?" Cass asked

as they got closer to the boxing gym entrance. "Poppa, I mean. He looks pretty serious in the photos."

Their house was practically a shrine to Poppa's legacy. Even though they'd never met their grandpa, the boys would recognize his strong jaw and steely glare anywhere.

"If he's anything like Dad, he'll want to know why I'm not in the ring every spare minute," Micah said.

Cass slapped his brother on the shoulder. "I hear you. Dad is obsessed with turning you into the family's next boxing champ."

Micah sighed. "Don't get me wrong, boxing once a week is fun. But it's nothing compared to how I feel when I'm designing supercars in my sketchbook."

They had arrived at the boxing gym's imposing metal door. Just as they reached for the handle, the door swung open.

The boys stepped back as a giant of a man lumbered through the dark doorway. He had a shaved head and his dark brown skin was slick with sweat. He mopped his brow with a towel that was slung over his shoulder.

For once in their lives, the two boys were speechless. There was no mistaking it – this was Poppa, although he looked older than in his Olympic champion photos.

Poppa raised one eyebrow. If he was shocked to see two kids gawping at him like silent frogs, he didn't show it. "Shouldn't you gentlemen be at school?" he

asked, before taking a swig from his water bottle.

He sounded like their dad. Even though it only felt like a few hours since they had left for school, Micah and Cass felt a twinge of homesickness.

"Um … we … I mean … errr," stuttered Cass.

Micah grimaced. It had been easy to *decide* to tell Poppa the truth – but now that he was about to actually tell him, he knew how ridiculous it would sound. He took a deep breath. "Basically, we're your grandkids from the future, Cass and Micah, and we're here to save the world from an evil genius called Noel Riche, but his daughter is chasing us and—"

"Steady on!" Poppa chuckled. "Do I look like I'm old enough to be someone's grandpa?"

"Not *now*. We're from the future," Cass said. "And we can prove it!"

Poppa crossed his arms. A smile danced on his lips. He clearly thought this was a joke. "Now this I would like to hear."

Micah recited the facts he knew about his grandpa. Thanks to spending a childhood surrounded by his achievements, he knew them off by heart: "During your career, you had seventy-eight wins including twenty-two knockouts," he blurted out. "You won gold at the 1976 Montreal Olympics wearing your lucky gold chain, which was a gift from Granny ... I mean, your wife."

Poppa was amused. "That's all common knowledge. If you are going to convince me that you are my future grandsons, you need to do better than that."

"We know about your birthmark!" Cass said. "The mole on ... you know. We have it too."

Poppa's smile faded. "How do you know about the family birthmark?"

"That's not all we know about," Micah said. "We have something to show you. Cass?"

"Micah?"

"Show Poppa our proof."

"Oh, right. Sure." Cass checked his pockets. "Um."

"Come on, Cass. The medal," hissed Micah.

Cass's cheeks flushed. He patted down the pockets of his blazer, but he already knew the truth. "I don't have it," he mumbled. "Maybe I dropped it at the arcade when we were crawling around the floor."

The brothers felt awful. Not only had they lost their evidence, and any chance of persuading their grandpa to help them, but they had also lost his precious Olympic medal.

Poppa clapped his hands together. His smile was back in place. "Thank you for amusing me on my break, but I have work to do. If you ever want boxing lessons, you know where to find me."

"You can't go!" Micah yelled. "If you don't help us, we can't complete our mission."

"I enjoy a joke as much as the next man, but I think it's best you get back to school," Poppa said firmly.

TOOT-TOOT!

A car horn caught their attention and the three of them turned.

"Frank!" Cass said with delight.

Micah never thought he'd be happier to see the old banger.

The car pulled up outside and rolled down the passenger seat window. *"I think you forgot something pretty vital, boys,"* Frank said.

There on the front passenger seat was the Olympic gold medal.

8

Cass picked up the gold medal and held it high, as triumphant as if he had won it himself. "See! Told you we were from the future. How else would we have *this*!" He presented it to Poppa with a flourish.

Poppa squinted at the medal. "How the devil did you get hold of this?"

"Do you believe us now, Grandpa?" Micah asked hopefully.

"I believe that there is a thief on the loose," Poppa huffed. He walked over to Frank and tapped at the tinted windows. "Excuse me, driver, you have some explaining to do. This medal is private property!" He took in the car's rusty maroon paint and mismatched headlights. "This vehicle has certainly seen better days," he said to the boys.

"Excuse me! You try travelling through two temporal wormholes on a half-empty battery," Frank huffed. *"That journey would knock the stuffing out of any car."*

"Temporal what–now? I insist you get out of the car so we can have a real chat," Poppa said, "man to man."

"More like car to man," Cass snickered.

"That's not gonna happen," Micah said, patiently explaining. "Frank *is* the car. It's a driverless car from the future. Which is where we've come from too."

"MK-893000 at your service," Frank said. *"Or Frank for short. And I am more than a mere car. I*

am a carefully calibrated time travel machine. Watch this!"

The car's rusty maroon exterior shimmered into invisibility before their eyes.

It was the single coolest thing any of them had ever seen. But it only lasted a few seconds.

Frank popped back into sight.

"Where did you go?!" Poppa demanded.

"I didn't go anywhere," Frank said. *"I activated Camo Mode. One million tiny reflective cameras turn on and reflect the space around the vehicle, thus giving the illusion of invisibility,"* he said proudly.

"That. Is. Genius!" Micah said.

"You should know, Young Micah," Frank said. *"You are the co-inventor of it."*

Micah's mouth fell open. "Me?" he gasped. "I am? I mean, I will be?"

The fact that Micah would invent something so mind-blowingly amazing? Well, it kind of blew *his* mind a little.

Micah looked over at Poppa, who was leaning back against the wall in stunned silence.

"Um, Grandpa? You all right?" Cass asked. "I know it's a lot to take in."

Their grandpa seemed shaken. "I think you boys should come inside after all," he said slowly. "I've got a few questions for you."

Micah and Cass squished on to the battered sofa in Poppa's office. Apart from a small framed newspaper clipping announcing his gold medal, you'd never know he was an Olympic champion. Their grandpa made himself a cup of tea with honey in it and handed them cups of orange squash.

"Go on then," said Poppa, dropping into a chair behind his desk. "Tell me everything. Not saying I'll believe you, but you can tell me."

They finally began their prepared speech from earlier and brought Poppa up to date. They told him everything about their mission – how they would stop Noel Riche from turning into a supervillain and ruling the world by befriending him as a child. Poppa listened carefully, nodding from time to time. When they finished, he was silent.

"So, Grandpa, what do you reckon?" Micah asked.

He squinted at them from behind his desk, sipping his tea. "If you boys are *really* from the future, can you tell me if Skylark wins the Grand National next weekend or not?"

"What's the Grand National?" Cass asked.

"It's a big horse race," Micah said. "And even if we did know which horse won, we couldn't tell you. That wouldn't be ethical."

"Humph. I don't see why you can't help your old grandpa out," Poppa sniffed.

"Our future selves said we can only share essential information," Micah said.

"That's true," Cass piped up. "It's on a strictly need-to-know basis."

"I suppose you can't tell me anything about our family in the future either? Who the next generation of boxers in our family might be?" Poppa leaned forward, his eyes shining. "Boxing runs in your blood, doesn't it?"

"Sorry, Grandpa," Micah said. He was starting to realize that this time-travelling business could get complicated. "We can only talk about our mission."

Poppa sighed. "So let me get this straight. You need to find this Noel character and help him push back against these bullies. Teach him there are other ways to stand up for yourself beyond wreaking world destruction."

Micah nodded. "Yep. Which might be harder than it sounds because Noel Riche looks like a right nerd. I bet he makes it easy for the bullies."

"No one deserves to be bullied, my boy," said Poppa sharply. "And I wouldn't make fun of how people look either. No, this Noel Riche clearly has immense intellect — we just need to make sure it is channelled in the right way. What do you need from me?"

"Our future selves didn't really say how you could help exactly. Although they suggested we use the boxing gym as a base. So I guess by giving us a place to stay?" Micah said. "Who knows how long this mission will take."

"Yeah! And maybe you could provide food for the mission too. It's well past lunchtime," Cass said. "Time travel is hungry work."

Poppa smiled. "I can certainly provide food and shelter. But let's get one thing straight: if anyone hears you call me 'grandpa', it would prove very confusing. From now on, call me Uncle Femi."

Micah nodded. "Got it, Uncle Femi."

A crackling sound interrupted them. It appeared to come from Micah's blazer.

"Boys, can you hear me?" said a familiar voice.

"It's Frank! On the walkie-talkie pin," Micah said.

Poppa shook his head. "Wow, future technology really is something. It's just like a spy film."

Micah lifted his blazer lapel up and spoke into the hidden mic. "We can hear you, Frank. What's up?"

"I've hidden around the corner but I can see our new friends are right outside the boxing gym!"

Micah and Cass shot up from their seats.

Cass gasped. "How did they find us so quickly?"

"Grandpa— I mean Uncle Femi, we need a place to hide! Those people outside in that fancy supercar have been looking for us since we left 2023!" Micah said.

"Who is in this supercar? Should I be concerned?" Poppa asked.

"Noel Riche sent his snotty daughter and her chauffeur to follow us into the past and sabotage our mission," Micah said.

"Believe me, I know Noelle and that blighter Grunton will stop at nothing to save the Richecorp empire," Frank said through the walkie-talkie.

"I think they're going door-to-door looking for us. Poppa, is there anywhere we can hide?" Micah asked.

Poppa leaped from his chair and opened the office door. "Quick! Take the fire escape stairs up to the roof. I will let you know when it's safe to come down."

Micah and Cass didn't have to be told twice. They ran up the staircase and didn't stop until they reached the roof. They were on the run – again.

9

Even from three storeys up in the air, Micah and Cass could hear Noelle and the chauffeur on the pavement down below. Micah was right: they were knocking on doors, asking neighbours if they'd seen the boys.

On the other side of the gym, Frank was parked between the rubbish bins and away from crowds.

Frank's voice came through the walkie-talkie pin. *"Stay low and out of sight until I say so. Over and out."*

Micah took off his blazer and tied the arms around his waist. It was far too hot for school uniform.

"Micah, look! Isn't that our school?" Cass pointed to a squat grey building on the other side of the road. It was so close they could see maths equations on the blackboard through the windows.

"Yeah! It's just missing the new science block," he said.

"This is our chance to get into school and find Noel. It's Friday and if we don't track him down now, we won't see him till Monday." He dug out his phone, but the screen was blank – maybe it didn't work at all in 1985. "Frank, what's the time?"

"Fourteen hundred hours, fifteen minutes and eleven seconds," Frank said. *"Greenwich Mean Time."*

"So, assuming school finishes at 3.15 p.m. in

1985, we have an hour before it shuts and we lose track of Noel," Micah said. "We need to be at Eastbrook the second the gates open."

Cass squinted in the sunlight. "It can't be more than fifty metres away. I can see the assembly hall windows from here!"

"I've got an idea, fellas. I might just be able to activate Heli Mode," Frank said.

Cass gasped. "You're a helicopter too?! That's so cool!"

"Now you tell us!" Micah said. "Come rescue us, then!"

Frank gave a wheezing laugh. *"Steady on, boys. I do not in fact convert into a helicopter, but I do have a flying contraption somewhere in this boot. It's a bit rusty, but it should work. Give me a second."*

Micah and Cass slowly, carefully, peeked over the wall to see what was going on. They saw the burly chauffeur and Noelle getting closer to the gym. Even though the boys trusted Poppa to protect them, could he hold his own against Grunton?

"Frank, where's that helicopter?" Micah yelled.

"Hang on, just looking – yes! Knew I still had it in the trunk. Two parachutes coming your way," Frank said triumphantly.

The boys peeked over and saw the car's sunroof had peeled back.

"Watch your 'eads!"

What looked like two rockets launched from Frank's sunroof and shot high into the air … and landed on the roof of the neighbouring building.

"Did it work?" Frank asked breathlessly.

"Yeah, it worked great. If we were on the building next door," Micah muttered.

"Can you try again, Frank?" Cass pleaded. He peeked over the roof's wall. "Noelle and Grunton are still down there!"

"Sorry, lads, those were my only parachutes. I think my targeting is a bit skew-whiff on account of my low battery."

"Recharge, then!" Micah yelled.

"I can't — my recharging station is in the year 2045. My battery has to last the mission," Frank said.

The boys looked around frantically. The completely flat rooftop had no hiding spots and the only route off it was the fire escape they had come up.

"We could hide here until Grunton and Noelle drive away?" Cass said.

"That could take ages!" Micah said. "If we're going to find Noel Riche, we need to be on the school grounds before it closes for the weekend."

Cass sighed. "Then we need to find a way off this roof ASAP."

"Frank, do you have a trampoline we don't know about?" Micah said desperately.

"No trampoline, I'm afraid!"

"So we can't jump," Micah sighed.

Cass's eyes lit up. "I have an idea. But it's risky."

"Tell me!" Micah said. "It's got to be better than being caught by Noelle and failing the mission."

"We can't jump. But we can zip line!" Cass said.

"Huh?!" Micah said.

Cass pointed to the electric cables on tall wooden poles dotted around the neighbourhood. "They're everywhere! And this one leads straight down into the school playing field."

The pole was rooted to the pavement, but the tip of it was next to the roof edge. Cass ran over to the pole and took off his blazer. He closed his eyes and took a deep breath. "

Pretend it's the zip line in the playground," he whispered to himself. Then he shimmied up the wooden pole with his blazer slung over one arm.

"Cass, stop!" Micah yelled. "Do you know how long I'll be grounded for if you get electrocuted? I may as well never leave 1985!"

"Blazers don't conduct electricity, Micah!" Cass said. "Don't you listen in science?"

Before Micah could stop him, Cass swung the blazer over the cable and grabbed both sleeves firmly. "See you on the other side!" he yelled before flying down the cable at an alarming speed.

Micah gulped. Then he climbed up the wooden pole and followed his brother down the cable.

"Woohoo!" Micah yelled. The city flew by in a blur as he soared down the pole, holding tight to the sleeves of his blazer.

But then Micah realized he couldn't stop. And the wooden pole in the schoolyard was getting closer and closer and—

"Argh!" Micah groaned as he smacked

straight into the pole and tumbled into a nearby hedge.

"Cass! Where are you?" Micah hissed, staggering on to all fours. All he could see was green and brown.

He felt a sharp tug on his leg. Before he knew it, he was being dragged out of the hedge.

"Wasn't that awesome?" said Cass, his face glowing with excitement. "Best fun I've had in ages."

"Yeah, awesome," muttered Micah, picking leaves out of his hair. "Except for the near-death part." But he found himself smiling. That *had* been fun. "That was a good idea there, Cass. We'd still be stuck up that roof without you. Who knew a school uniform could be so useful?"

Frank's concerned voice fizzled through their walkie-talkie. *"Boys, are you there?"*

"We made it, Frank!" Cass said.

Micah dusted a few twigs off his back. He

saw a familiar concrete path leading to stubby grey buildings. They had made it to Eastbrook Secondary.

"How do we find Noel?" Micah asked. "We don't know what class he's in."

"Well, he was eleven in 1985. Which means that he's in Year 7 – that should narrow it down a bit," Cass said.

Micah nodded. "Let's wait by the school gate at home time. He's bound to come out eventually. We can meet him and finally get somewhere with this mission."

They began walking towards the heavy iron gates, looking over their shoulders to check they weren't being followed.

"It's hardly changed," Micah said.

Cass nodded. "Just like we never left. Why do I feel like we're skiving?"

"Because that is precisely what you are doing," said a voice.

The boys turned around. A teacher in a grey skirt suit was looking down her nose at them.

"What are you doing in this school? You are not wearing Eastbrook Secondary uniform!"

"S-sorry, miss," Cass stuttered.

Her eyes narrowed. "Who are you?" she barked.

"W-we're new," said Micah, thinking fast. "Our records are being sent over. That's why we're not in class; we weren't sure where to go."

"And we don't have our new uniforms yet!" Cass added.

"Being new is no excuse," the teacher said with a scowl. "You'd better come with me."

Micah and Cass had no choice but to follow.

10

The scowling teacher was called Mrs Franklin and she made Mr Rankford seem like a cuddly teddy bear. Mrs Franklin gave Micah and Cass detention for two "misdemeanours", as she put it: skipping lessons and having completely the wrong uniform.

It turned out that the uniform at Eastbrook Secondary in 1985 was very different to the uniform in 2023. In a sea of maroon blazers, grey trousers and dorky-looking peaked caps, Micah and Cass stuck out in their dark blue blazers, black trousers and bare heads.

It was going to make blending in *impossible*.

"Sit here and think about what you've done," Mrs Franklin said, ushering the boys into a stuffy classroom full of miserable-looking students and a sleepy-looking teacher. "I hope to see you on Monday with a better attitude!"

So, while every other student at Eastbrook was heading towards freedom, Micah and Cass were forced to sit in silence behind worn wooden desks. Micah looked out of the window, hoping to spot Noel Riche in the flood of students. But it was no use. There were too many students and he barely remembered what Noel Riche looked like anyway.

Their mission was ruined before it had even begun.

"Oi, Micah. Is detention always this boring?" Cass whispered.

"Quiet, boys," muttered the teacher. He didn't even look up from his newspaper.

Micah shrugged. "Never had it before."

The teacher's newspaper crumpled. "No talking in detention! Or you *all* stay later."

The other kids gave Micah and Cass death stares. This was way more attention than they needed.

Micah flushed. *Great, now the other kids hate us,* he thought.

The rest of the children slumped over their desks, doodling in exercise books or pretending to read battered paperbacks. The arms of the clock moved as slow as treacle. It was like time had paused in the little classroom.

The teacher looked as bored as the students. He walked slowly between the desks with both arms behind his back. He paused at Micah's desk.

"Where is your exercise book?" he demanded.

"I … forgot it?" Micah said.

The teacher sighed wearily. "I suggest you go to your locker and fetch it, then. Quickly!"

Micah wasn't about to argue. He shot out of the classroom and glanced back at the door only to see Cass mouthing "traitor" at him.

He walked slowly through the empty school halls, keeping his eyes peeled for Noel Riche (maybe he did some sort of after-school club) or his fiendish future daughter.

As he walked past rows of metal lockers, he realized he still had the envelope his future self had left for them – he'd tucked it inside his blazer pocket. He took it out. There was something heavy in there. They had used the ten pence coin at the arcade, so that only left—

"The key!" he exclaimed.

Micah rummaged in the envelope until he felt it: a sharp corner. The rusty key was too small to be for a car or a front door.

But it might just work for a locker.

What if Future Micah and Future Cass had left their next clue right here, in the school?

But there was a problem. There were hundreds of lockers in this corridor, let alone the rest of the school. Micah couldn't try each one; he'd be there all night and well into the weekend.

Micah looked closer at the old key. It was stained by something like ink or black paint. He rinsed the key under a nearby water fountain, then polished it with a corner of his blazer.

Slowly but surely, a pattern emerged on the key head. It looked like a series of circles and lines. He wiped it again and all became clear. They were numbers!

"Three, nine, five," he said to himself.

He looked up. Every single locker in the hall was numbered. He stood between lockers 187 and 189.

Micah broke into a grin. He knew his future self would have his back.

When Cass was finally released from detention,

Micah was waiting for him by the school entrance.

"Pssst! Cass, over here!" he hissed from around the corner.

Cass strode over to him with a face like thunder. "Bro, you totally abandoned me! And Mr Froggart is well annoyed that you didn't come back. Said you were going to get another misdemeanour, whatever that is."

Micah held up a small duffel bag and smiled. "I had more important things to do. Like finding our next clue!"

He explained that the key in the envelope had been for a school locker. And that locker contained a duffel bag with Eastbrook uniforms in their size.

"Check it out! There are blazers, trousers and those weird-looking caps. All in the right colour," Micah said. "We're going to fit in fine now!"

Cass crossed his arms. "So we've got a ridiculous uniform like all the other kids. Anything else? You know, something to help us save the world?"

Micah deflated. "I don't think so," he admitted.

"Are you sure they didn't leave us anything else? Like a real gadget?" Cass asked, rummaging through the duffel bag.

"Nah. Just the clothes."

"Perfect," Cass muttered. "It's the weekend so we don't even need them. What do we do next? We've missed Noel, we don't know where he lives, and we can't go back to the boxing gym any time soon."

Micah spoke into his lapel walkie-talkie. "Frank, can you pick us up? We need to decide our next move."

"Roger that, young Micah," Frank said. "Over and out."

"And meet us by the back gates," Cass added. "The last thing we need is Frank making us look even *more* out-of-place."

They walked across the schoolyard, which was now completely empty and quiet.

"Wow. It's dead," Cass said.

"It's a hot Friday afternoon. Why would anyone want to stick around at school?"

Micah imagined all the things he'd be doing if he was back home. Getting ready for boxing lessons with Dad, probably, and wishing he was pottering around a garage instead.

Still, he'd rather be in the gym than be pursued by the daughter of a supervillain who was trying to stop them from saving the world.

Suddenly, a short maroon and grey blur whizzed past them and sprinted towards the school's back gates. The blur was a young boy and he was running as fast as his legs would carry him.

"Someone's keen to get home," Micah chuckled.

Cass nodded. "Yeah. Poor kid probably had detention too." He paused. "Hey, Micah, you don't think…"

Just as the boy made it to the back gate, two other boys jumped out of nowhere to block his path.

The bigger one sneered in his face. "Where do you think you're going, Noel?"

11

The boy called Noel had floppy brown hair, an oversized blazer and looked like a rabbit caught in the headlights. He looked exactly like his school photo, down to the jam-jar glasses.

The brothers hurried over.

"I knew that boy looked familiar!" Cass said, elbowing Micah.

The two bullies looked up. "Oi! What are you weirdos looking at?" The bigger one said. He looked at least fourteen, had a funny-looking bowl haircut and towered over Micah.

Micah gulped. "Cass, just follow my lead. All right?"

Cass nodded.

Micah stood up straighter and plastered a fake smile on his face. "Noel, mate! We've been looking for you everywhere."

Noel looked utterly blank.

"Come on," said Micah. "We don't want to be late."

Noel nodded slowly. He still looked bewildered but was clearly sharp enough to play along. "Oh, right! Sorry I'm late," he said. He walked towards Micah and Cass, clutching his backpack straps tightly.

"Where d'ya think you're going, Nitwit Noel?" said the other bully said. He was a bit shorter than his friend, but still looked menacing. "You don't expect us to believe these are your friends, do you? We all know you haven't got any."

"Yeah. Why else do you spend so much time in the library after school?"

Noel froze.

"Yo, Noel. Our uncle's waiting for us all outside. He's taking us on a tour of Champion's Boxing Gym, remember?" Cass said. "You know he trains there, right?" He let his gaze wander casually to the other boys. "He's a champion boxer. Won an Olympic medal. Heavyweight."

A flash of fear flickered in the bully's eyes and he stepped backwards.

The two older boys picked up their backpacks. "This ain't over," one of them hissed in Noel's ear as he walked away.

When the older boys were out of sight, Micah and Cass burst into relieved laughter.

"I can't believe it worked!" Micah said. "We found him!"

Noel squinted at Micah. "What do you mean, you *found me*? Who are you, anyway?"

Micah and Cass exchanged glances. They had tried so hard to find Noel Riche, but they hadn't at any point decided what they would say once they found him.

After a tense silence, Micah spoke up: "We saw what was going on and wanted to help. If you turn and face the other way when someone is being bullied, you might as well be the bully too," he said. "Something my dad always says."

Cass thought back to that morning when Micah's friends had teased Cass about his Rubik's Cube. He wished Micah had spoken up then.

Noel loosened his grip on his backpack.

"Well, it was very nice of you," he said. "Thanks." He began to walk off.

The brothers looked at each other, panicked. Losing Noel was *not* part of the plan.

"Wait, Noel!" Micah said, stalling for time. "Have you built any … er … cool rockets lately?"

Noel whipped round and looked at them suspiciously. "How did you know about my rockets?" He frowned. "And why haven't I seen you at school before?"

"We're, um, new," said Micah. "That's why we haven't got the right uniform yet."

"Yeah, we're starting school here properly on Monday," said Cass.

"Really?" said Noel, still looking suspicious. "What class?"

Luckily for Micah and Cass, a clunking and thumping sound interrupted them. It came from the street.

"What is that racket?" Cass said.

Micah smirked. "What do you think?"

Frank pulled up to the back gate in all his rusty, mismatched glory. How could this car look even older than it did a few hours ago?

"What is *that*?" Noel gasped.

"It's our car," Cass said. "I know he, I mean *it*, has seen better days."

"What are you talking about? It's totally awesome!" Noel said. "I've never seen tyres like that before. I bet it goes really fast. You can tell by the aerodynamic design."

Somehow, Noel had looked past Frank's blemished exterior and seen the potential.

"It's even cooler on the inside," Micah grinned. "Wanna check it out?"

It turned out Noel was an even bigger car nerd than Micah, something that he had never thought possible. Noel wasn't put off by Frank's ramshackle appearance. In fact, he was super impressed by the futuristic rubber–steel hybrid tyres, the video screens in the seat headrests and, most importantly, the fact it was powered by artificial intelligence.

Luckily for Micah and Cass, Frank kept quiet. Noel could accept a self-driving car, it seemed, but a talking car might have been a step too far. And their time travel mission was meant to be a secret, after all.

"I can't believe it. A genuine self-driving car! It's almost as cool as *Knight Rider*," Noel said, gazing around the exterior in awe.

"*Knight Rider*?" Cass asked.

"You know, the TV show about the crime-fighting talking car. I thought everyone with a pulse watched *Knight Rider*," Noel snorted.

"Well, we don't have a TV," Micah said quickly.

"You have a self-driving car but no TV?" Noel said.

Micah realized he would have to tread carefully around this boy. He didn't miss a trick.

"Yeah, our parents are funny like that. How about we go for a spin?" Micah said.

Noel turned bright pink with joy. "Really? But don't we need a grown-up?"

"What for?" Cass said. "The car is voice activated!"

Micah sat in the front passenger seat while Noel and Cass sat in the back seat. Noel was too excited by the automated seat belts to care about the worn leather and hodge-podge fabrics.

Frank revved his engine and took them on a slow drive.

"Hey, Frank," Micah whispered into the walkie-talkie mic on his lapel. "Where are you taking us?"

"The scenic route, young Micah. The boxing gym still ain't safe," Frank said in hushed tones. *"We need to lay low until the coast is clear."*

In the back seat, Noel was giving Cass a tour of the neighbourhood. "There's the arcade where I have the fifth highest score on *Donkey Kong*! And this place does the best triple cheese pizza around," Noel said. "Or so everyone at school says."

Micah glanced outside the window and saw a familiar sign: *Awesome Pizza*.

"Hey, Micah," Cass piped up from the back seat. "I think we've heard good things about *Awesome Pizza*." He gave an exaggerated wink.

"Huh?" Micah was blank for a second. Then he remembered.

The receipt in the envelope!

He carefully opened it and pulled out the faded receipt. Sure enough, it had the same *Awesome Pizza* logo at the top. Plus, there was a crumpled five pound note.

Could that be where their next clue was hiding? Or even, finally, a super-cool futuristic gadget?

"Don't know about you lot, but I'm starving," Micah said. "How about we stop for a slice of pizza?"

"I don't have enough money for pizza right now," Noel said nervously.

"Don't worry, mate. It's our treat!" Cass said. "Triple cheese it is!"

12

Micah, Cass and Noel stepped into the pizza parlour. It was full of older kids and families enjoying their meals. The scent of freshly baked bread and herbs reminded the brothers that their last meal had been breakfast – technically, that was thirty-eight years in the future.

Cass's eyes were as wide as the pizza ovens. "Oh, boy! I'm gonna get an extra-large triple cheese pizza and a berry shake and garlic bread and..."

"Calm down, bro! I only have five quid," Micah said. "We can only get one slice each."

Noel squeezed into a corner booth and looked around. "This place is even cooler on the inside," he said with a smile.

"You've never been here before?" Micah asked.

Noel shook his head. "I don't have many friends, and my family doesn't really go out for meals together. And … well, it isn't the sort of place you'd come alone."

Micah felt a little sorry for Noel. Micah had his mates at school, but they weren't really friends, exactly – just people he hung out with to avoid being alone. At least he always had Cass.

Micah and Cass joined the queue to order while Noel sat patiently in the booth.

"What do you think we should do next?" Micah asked.

"I reckon an *Awesome Pizza* combo meal.

Have you seen the prices on this menu? It's, like, one pound fifty for a large pizza!" Cass said. "There are some definite plus sides to the past."

Micah rolled his eyes. "I meant, what should we do with Noel?!"

"We stopped him from being bullied back at the school, didn't we?" Cass said.

"Yeah. But that wasn't the main incident. Remember when we watched Noel Riche's broadcast?"

"Like it was this morning," Cass smirked as they shuffled forward in the queue.

"Very funny," Micah said. "Well, Noel Riche said that the bullies threw stones at him because of his space rocket. And I don't remember seeing any stones earlier. Whatever turned Noel Riche into a vengeful, power-hungry scientist, it hasn't happened yet."

"You're right," Cass said. "He hasn't told anyone about his space rockets yet either, by the sound of it. Looks like we still have a mission to complete."

They got to the counter to place their order. It turned out that five pounds was exactly enough for three pizzas.

"Two large triple cheese pizzas, please," Micah said at the counter. "And I will have a large yellow pizza. Three-quarters pineapple, one-quarter sweetcorn and no tomato sauce."

The woman behind the counter smiled. "Funny, you're the second person to order that pizza today. Never heard of it before!"

"You mean someone ordered the same nasty pizza as him?" Cass said.

"Yes, around lunchtime. He was a lot older than you, though. Funny haircut," she said. "He sat on that stool by the window."

"What a coincidence," Micah muttered to Cass as they walked back to their booth.

Cass shook his head. "*Is* it a coincidence,

though? First there was the top score at the arcade with the same initials as me. Then the same yellow pizza order as you."

"What do you think it means?" Micah asked.

"It sounds kinda silly, but maybe our future selves are closer than we think. Like, they were just here," said Cass.

"I wish that were true, bro. Then we could leave this mission up to them and go back home where we belong," Micah said.

But Cass had a hunch. He marched over to the stool by the window and checked under the table. A few people stared as he ran his hand under the tabletop.

His fingers hit something hard.

"I knew it!" Cass said. He tugged at the sticky tape securing whatever-it-was to the table and tore it free.

His excitement dropped as fast as it had peaked. It was nothing but a stack of twigs.

Well, not quite twigs, but neatly trimmed sticks of wood.

Cass trudged back to the booth just as the pizzas arrived.

"Find anything?" Micah asked.

He shook his head. "Nah. Just these sticks."

Noel's eyes lit up. "You mean you don't want them?!"

"What am I gonna do with these, start a campfire?" Cass snorted. "You're welcome to them, Noel."

As if Cass was going to change his mind, Noel grabbed the sticks fast and shoved them in his backpack.

"Whoa! What's so special about those sticks?" Micah said.

Noel took a hungry bite of his pizza slice. "Balsa wood isn't cheap and my parents won't pay for it." He sighed. "So I need it to finish my science project. The assembly is on Monday."

"What's your science project, Noel?" Micah asked.

Noel stared at him. "You really want to know? Because no one *ever* asks me about my science projects – not even my mum or dad. They think my projects are a waste of time."

Micah smiled. "'Course! If you're this excited about it, it must be cool."

Noel dropped the pizza and took a giant black

notebook out of his rucksack. He opened the book, which took up most of the table.

Noel flicked through page after page of intricate-looking designs penned in black ink.

"Wait, what are these?" Cass asked, pointing to the designs.

"Oh, nothing. Just some of my more silly ideas. Like, imagine if you could play video games using a small handheld device that was totally wireless. It could work anywhere in the world! You could even play on the bus."

"Video games on the bus? Imagine that." Micah smiled.

Noel shrugged. "I know, it's pretty unlikely. But this is the project I'm *really* excited about."

Micah and Cass took in the image before them. It was the blueprint of a rocket that looked eerily familiar to both boys. The last time they had seen it, it had been pointed straight at their school.

"I'm building space rockets!" Noel pushed his glasses back up his nose, his eyes shining. "Not real ones, of course. Mine are made from wood and glue. But they are perfectly to scale. And I'm ninety-nine per cent certain that the science is accurate."

"It's the same rocket," Cass muttered under his breath.

Noel laughed. "I assure you, Cass, that nothing like my rocket has ever existed," he said. There was a confidence in his voice now and his shyness had gone.

Noel knew his stuff. And he *knew* that he knew his stuff.

"Oh, I can believe that," Micah said. "And I'm sure the, um, science is accurate." *So accurate it had reduced Mr Rankford's car to vapour*, he thought. "What will it do?"

"*Do?* What do you think?" Noel said. "It's going into space, of course! My rockets will send machinery to the furthest edges of our solar system! It will explore the unexplored and answer the unanswered! It will—"

"Wait! Let me get this straight," Cass said, "your rockets are going *into* space, to explore stuff? You wouldn't, say, launch them at the Earth?"

"Of course not! Why would I aim a rocket at the Earth?" Noel shook his head. "That would be really dangerous. People could get hurt. I'm not some kind of Bond villain." He laughed before taking another slice of pizza.

Micah and Cass chuckled nervously.

"Have you ever shown your rocket designs to anyone at school?" Micah asked.

Noel shook his head. "No one at school really gets it. But that all changes on Monday!"

Micah dropped his pizza slice. "What happens on Monday?"

"Show and tell assembly, duh!" Noel said

cheerfully. "Mrs Franklin has been talking about it all term."

"The whole school will see my rocket display. It's going to be totally awesome!"

Micah and Cass didn't have to say anything to each other. It was suddenly so obvious.

This was it. The assembly that would change Noel Riche's life for ever. It was three days away.

And they had to stop it from happening.

"Noel, mate, are you sure showing your rocket at this assembly is such a good idea?" Micah asked.

Noel looked confused. But before he could answer, a buzzing sound pierced the air. It was Micah's walkie-talkie.

"MAYDAY! MAYDAY! Pursuers are on the loose," Frank said. *"You need to vamoose."*

Noel gasped. "Did your blazer just speak to you?!"

Micah and Cass leaped up from their seats.

"No time to explain! We need to move," Micah said.

They turned to the door, but something blocked the exit. Or, rather, someone.

It was Grunton.

13

The chauffeur scanned the packed restaurant. It wasn't long before his eyes landed on Micah and Cass. When he did see them, he didn't yell, shout or chase.

He smiled. It was the worst smile that any of them had ever seen. They felt frozen to the spot, as though they were in a trance.

"Who is this guy?" Noel asked nervously.

"No time for questions!" Frank yelled through the walkie-talkie. *"Escape out back. Quickly!"*

The chauffeur took a slow step towards them, which finally kicked the boys into gear.

"This way!" Micah yelled, ushering his brother and Noel through a door that led into the kitchen.

"Oi! No customers in the kitchen!" yelled the woman behind the counter.

A wall of heat and steam greeted them in the cramped kitchen. Micah spun frantically, looking for the way out. There had to be one. He'd rather hide in the giant pizza cookers than face *him*.

"My notebook!" Noel gasped and he flung himself back through the doors.

"Come back right now!" Micah screamed in his bossiest voice. He had to make sure he and his little bro completed the mission in one piece.

"Oh my gosh, that boy is gonna get us killed," Cass groaned.

Luckily, Noel moved like his life depended on it. He raced to the booth, picked up his notebook and ran back through the kitchen.

Micah peered through the porthole window in the door. Not only was the chauffeur lumbering through the restaurant, but Noelle was right next to him.

"They're escaping!" she yelled.

A gust of fresh air moved through the kitchen. One of the cooks left through the back door, leaving it wide open.

The three boys ran towards their only exit, narrowly dodging angry cooks. The back door opened on to a narrow alleyway lined with giant rubbish bins.

"Let me through, you swine!" yelled a familiar voice. It was Noelle.

"What now, Frank?!" Cass panted.

"On your left!" Frank said through the walkie-talkie. *"The alley is too narrow for me to drive down!"*

The boys ran through the alley, hopping over rubbish bags and wheelie bins in an attempt to reach Frank.

Their beloved car pulled up to the road and the doors flew open.

Micah shot into the back seat, followed by Noel. Cass prepared to leap into the driver's seat but tripped on his shoe laces, tumbling to the ground.

When he got up, he felt a hand on his blazer collar.

Cass turned. He was face to face with Noelle, her cheeks rosy with the exertion of running. Her brown eyes blazed triumphantly and a single strand of hair had come loose from her immaculate ponytail. Grunton grabbed him and lifted him up.

He tried to wriggle free from Grunton's iron grip. "Let me go!"

Noelle laughed and it sounded like rusty nails in a tin can. "No one messes with my inheritance! You're not going any-WHOAHHH!"

It happened too quickly for Cass to register. He felt something loop around his waist and yank him into the air like a yo-yo. In a split second, he was in the car and secured tightly to his seat.

The car doors slammed shut and Frank zoomed away at breakneck speed. The car sped through the streets, dodging the traffic with ease. In a matter of seconds, they left the local high street behind and headed towards the motorway.

"What just happened?" Cass said. He looked down to see a seat belt tucked tightly around him.

"*I saved your life, young Cass, that's what!*" Frank said, with a hoarse cough. "*Don't expect me to activate my seat belt extension feature again. It drains my battery.*"

"Cass, who are you talking to?" Noel demanded. "And why were those people chasing us?!"

"*Cripes,*" Frank muttered. "*I forgot we had a guest.*"

"This is no ordinary car," Micah said. "We can't say more than that!"

"Nope! Not good enough. There's something

fishy about you guys," Noel said. Then he gasped and clutched his notebook tighter to his chest. "Is this corporate espionage? You're trying to steal my rocket designs, aren't you? That's why you were asking all those questions!"

"Chill, bro," Cass said. "We don't want your notebook."

"Listen, if we wanted your notebook we could have taken it at any time," Micah said.

"That's true," Noel said, considering. "But you *are* hiding something."

Before Micah could answer, they were all thrown forwards in their seats. Something jolted the car. The boys craned their necks to look out of the smashed back windscreen.

The silver supercar was on their tail. Again.

"Doesn't she ever give up?" wailed Micah.

"Frank, are you seeing this?!" Cass yelled.

"For the last time, who is Frank?" Noel shouted.

"*I'm Frank!*" yelled the car. "*Now will you stop bleedin' shouting so I can concentrate on escaping?*"

Noel looked stunned. "A talking car? This is better than any spy movie!"

Noelle popped her head out of the passenger seat window. She was clad in giant goggles to protect her eyes from the blistering winds generated at such high speeds. She pulled something gleaming and silver out of the supercar, and aimed it at Frank with deadly focus.

Noel squinted. "She's got a crossbow! Where are your weapons and gadgets?"

"Don't ask," Cass muttered. It was still a sore subject that, so far, their future selves had left them with nothing more advanced than a walkie-talkie.

"*They may have the shinier gadgets, but I am one step ahead,*" Frank said. "*Activate Iron Wheels!*"

The boys felt a slight thud just as Noelle took aim at the ground beneath the car.

"Guys, she's gonna shoot! And we're gonna crash!" Micah yelled.

Cass braced his head in the recovery position. Noel said a silent prayer.

THWACK!

Noelle shot a silver arrow at Frank's tyres. Nothing happened.

She released a volley of arrows, one after the other. But they all bounced off the iron armour surrounding the tyres.

The expression on Noelle's face said it all – even behind the goggles, they knew the look she gave them was pure poison. She ducked back into the car.

"Well done, Frank!" Cass cheered.

"Let's not get too excited," Micah said. "They're still on our tail and they probably have more weapons up their sleeves. What are we gonna do?"

"We need a diversion!" Noel said. "Something

to distract them while we make a run for it."

"In case you didn't notice, Frank doesn't exactly blend in," Micah said. "We are going to stick out wherever we go."

"Young Noel has given me an idea," Frank said. *"Now, I know I have that protocol saved somewhere…"*

The supercar was so close that they could see Grunton grimacing through the windscreen.

"Make it quick, Frank!" Cass whimpered. "I'd like to make it back home with my spine intact!"

"Found it!" Frank yelled triumphantly. *"Activating Twin Mode."*

Nothing happened. At least, that's how it seemed.

"Frank, try again! It didn't work," Micah said.

"Look to your left, young Micah," Frank said smugly.

The boys turned to look out the window. Their jaws dropped.

"Th-th-that's us!" Cass stuttered.

A car that looked exactly like Frank, right down to the wonky headlights, peeling maroon paintwork and silver passenger door, was driving along the road beside them.

"Don't tell me another Frank exists," Micah said. "This is all too much for my brain."

"Not quite. Twin Mode creates a hologram duplicate that projects from a small camera on the roof," Frank said.

Noel gasped. "You're telling me *that's* a hologram?! It looks so real!"

"I bet Noelle and Grunton don't know what's hit 'em!" Cass said.

"Now for the pièce de résistance," Frank said. *"Hold on tight, kiddos!"*

"Woaaaaaah!" the boys screamed as the car took a sharp right turn and sped down a hill.

Frank's engine puttered to a stop at the bottom.

Micah watched from the back window as the holographic Frank raced down the road they'd just left, closely followed by the silver supercar. They had lost them.

"Am I still alive?" Cass said, his eyes still squeezed shut.

"Can we do that again?!" Micah said excitedly.

"Is *anyone* going to tell me why you have a talking car?" Noel said.

Micah and Cass looked at each other. They were going to have to give Noel some answers.

14

All the way back to the boxing gym, Noel wouldn't stop talking.

"Are you superheroes? FBI agents? Bounty hunters? Aliens sent from another galaxy? Are you—"

"Noel, if we tell you, will you shut up?" Micah yelled.

Noel nodded eagerly and pretended to zip his mouth shut.

"Bro, we can't say anything," Cass pleaded. "You know we can't. This could mess up the future for ever!"

Micah sighed. He remembered the warning from his future self: don't tell anyone why you're there except Poppa. He had no intention of telling Noel the whole truth. But he had to tell him *something*.

Micah sighed. "Earlier today, you asked if we were spies sent by a business to steal your designs. Well, you were half right."

Noel gasped. "I knew it!"

"We don't want to steal your designs. The opposite, in fact. We want to protect them from being stolen," Micah said. "Someone very important is after them."

"So you *are* spies?" Noel asked. "And that's why you have access to this awesome tech!"

"I can neither confirm nor deny that," Micah said.

Noel nodded seriously. "Don't worry, Agent Micah. Your secret's safe with me."

Cass breathed a silent sigh of relief. His brother's plan had worked.

Frank pulled up around the corner of Champion's Boxing Gym.

"Are you sure it's safe for us to return, Frank?" Cass asked. The memory of being pursued by Noelle and Grunton on the roof was still fresh in his mind.

"*I think so, Young Cass,*" Frank said. "*Noelle and Grunton should still be chasing a hologram.*"

"There's nowhere else for us to go, anyway," Micah said.

"*Keep your walkie-talkie mics close at all time, boys. I will patrol and alert you if that supercar gets close,*" Frank said.

The sun had set, but the gym was busier than ever. Men and women of all ages sipped water in-between bouts, and the sound of laughter rang down the street.

Cass squinted out of the window. "Hey,

Micah! Isn't that Mr Khan from the corner shop?"

"Oh yeah!" Micah said. Sure enough, a very young looking Mr Khan (minus the grey beard) chuckled with a group of friends as they sipped water outside the gym.

"What is this place?" Noel asked.

"It's our uncle's boxing gym – we weren't lying about that."

"Our uncle is the only one who knows about our mission," Cass said. "It's the safest place for us to be."

Noel clutched his notebook tighter. "Are you sure?"

"Just wait until you meet our Poppa! He was an Olympic champ, you know?" Micah said proudly.

"Poppa? I thought you said he was your uncle?" Noel asked.

"Er, it's a nickname we have. Runs in the family," Cass said quickly.

Micah, Cass and Noel left the car and walked into the brightly-lit boxing gym. Poppa leaped across the room when he saw them.

"Boys, you're safe!" he said, giving Micah and Cass a big hug. He turned to Noel. "You're not another relative I don't know about, are you?"

"No, sir," Noel said, rather nervously.

"This is our friend Noel from school," Cass said. He shot his grandpa a meaningful look.

"Ah, yes, of course." Poppa shook Noel's hand warmly. "Call me Uncle Femi. Or, er Poppa."

"This place is awesome," Noel said, looking around the boxing gym.

Micah had to admit, it did look pretty impressive. The wide hall was much bigger on the inside than it looked from the outside. Three boxing rings were spaced evenly throughout the hall and gleaming punching bags hung from the ceiling. There were lessons taking place and training sessions. Music from the radio speakers drifted over the sound of laughter and conversation.

Micah wished the boxing gym he went to was more like this one: fun and sociable instead of so *serious*. Dad seemed to think that boxing and laughter didn't mix. That there was no point in boxing if you didn't want to win. But the clients here seemed to be enjoying themselves as well as working hard.

"Thank you, Noel," Poppa said. "You are welcome to train here any time you like."

"I don't exactly have anyone to train with," Noel mumbled.

"Nonsense! Everyone who steps through the threshold of this gym is a friend and a brother," Poppa said. He turned to his grandsons. "Before I forget: have you had any trouble from our menacing friends?"

"Like you wouldn't believe!" Frank piped up through the walkie-talkie mic.

Poppa chuckled. "Step into my office and tell me all about it."

By the time Micah, Cass and Noel had filled in Poppa about their epic car chase, the boxing gym had mostly emptied out for the night. Employees stuck their heads round the door to say goodnight and Poppa waved each one off with a grin. He was much less intimidating than the boys had been led to believe.

Noel showed Poppa his rocket sketches. "This boy has talent!" Poppa exclaimed. "We have a budding genius on our hands."

Noel's cheeks turned pink with pride. He clearly wasn't used to being praised. "Mum and Dad think my drawings are a waste of time and that I should be studying instead," he mumbled.

Micah nodded. "I know the feeling. But you're so talented and it makes you happy, so don't give up."

"Do you really like them? I can't wait to demonstrate the rockets at Monday's assembly," Noel said, bouncing excitedly on his seat. "I've made a scaled-down model using ice lolly sticks and old newspaper."

Micah groaned. "Noel, mate, I don't think that's a good idea."

"Yeah," Cass jumped in. "Those bullies will never let you live it down."

Noel shrugged. "Those guys bother me whatever I do. I might as well do what I want."

Poppa shook his head. "Quite right, Noel!" He turned to look sternly at his grandsons. "I cannot believe what I am hearing! I sincerely hope no offspring of mine would ever dim their light because of a bully. Noel, you must share your passion with the world."

"Even if other people think it's stupid and childish?" Cass asked. The Rubik's Cube incident felt like a lifetime ago, but it was still fresh in his mind.

"Who cares what they think? If what you do brings you joy and does not cause any harm, then pursue it with pride," Poppa said. "Never forget that being a bully is a sign of weakness."

"We just don't want Noel to get hurt, Uncle Femi," Micah said. "Those bullies are always on his case."

"Maybe you could teach Noel how to defend himself?" Cass asked.

"Yeah! Show him how to land a strong right hook," Micah said.

Poppa rose out of the chair behind his desk. His tall frame suddenly seemed even more imposing. "I assure you that boxing is about more than landing a few punches," he said sternly. "It is as strategic and tactical as a game of chess."

"I never thought about it like that," Micah mumbled.

"Clearly it isn't just Noel who would benefit from my tutelage," Poppa said. "All three of you boys need boxing lessons. Noel, can you be here bright and early tomorrow morning?"

Noel nodded. "Yes, sir!"

Poppa smiled. "Good. That is when my boxing boot camp will begin."

15

"Rise and shine, boys!" Poppa bellowed cheerfully.

Micah and Cass opened their eyes. For one-tenth of a second, they thought they were back home in their own beds, with Dad frying plantain downstairs and Mum singing along (badly) with the radio.

Then the truth brought them crashing down to reality. They were nowhere near home. They were so far from home it wasn't even funny.

And they were really sore from a night spent sleeping on the floor of Poppa's office.

"It's still dark outside," Cass groaned.

Micah sat up and rubbed his eyes. "Just ten more minutes, Uncle Femi?"

Gone was the twinkly-eyed warm man from yesterday. In his place was a taskmaster.

"What do you think this is? A holiday? No, my boys. Boxing boot camp has begun. We begin with roadwork. Up you get!"

With impressive strength, Poppa hauled Micah and Cass out of their makeshift beds and on to their feet. He ushered them into the kitchen where they gulped down plain porridge (ick!) followed by an icy shower (aargh!) in the gym's changing rooms.

"Maybe we should have let Noelle and the chauffeur catch us after all," Cass whispered as they changed into grey T-shirts and tracksuit bottoms.

A sharp whistle interrupted their grumbling.

"Less of your belly-aching!" Poppa yelled. He was clearly in his element. "Or I'll add another ten minutes to your jog."

"He's worse than Dad," Micah groaned.

Both boys dragged themselves outside where Poppa stood next to a young girl they hadn't seen before. She was wearing sunglasses and a hoodie with the *Champion's Boxing Gym* logo on it, and couldn't have been more than ten.

"Micah and Cass, this is my protégé and niece Joanne," he said. "She will be my assistant during boot camp. Joanne, the boys are staying with me for the weekend, right here at the gym."

"Pleased to meet ya!" She grinned.

"Hngph," the boys grunted in return, wondering how she was so perky this early in the morning.

Poppa frowned. "Perhaps your manners will return after a one mile jog. Off you go!"

The boys had no choice but to run several laps around the boxing gym, while Joanne and Poppa whistled aggressively every time they slowed down.

"Hey, Micah," Cass panted. They were on their third lap around the block. "If Joanne is Poppa's niece then she must be Dad's cousin."

"You mean *that's* Aunty Joanne?!"

Micah and Cass knew Aunty Joanne as the aunt who put too much sherry into the Christmas trifle. It was nearly impossible for them to imagine her as the feisty ten-year-old girl with pigtails.

They finished their laps and Joanne threw them a bottle of water each. "Uncle Femi was right. You two really need this boot camp."

The boys were huffing and puffing too loudly to think of a comeback. When they finally caught their breath, Noel arrived at the boxing gym wearing what looked like his PE kit. Poppa ushered them into a private section of the gym, right at the back.

"So, when do we throw some punches?" Cass said excitedly.

"There's plenty of time for that. Today, we focus on building strength here and here," Poppa said, pointing to his forehead and then to his chest.

"You mean we're gonna learn how to headbutt?" Micah asked. He was pretty sure that was against the rules.

Joanne sighed. "No, silly. Uncle Femi means that boxing starts with mental and emotional strength."

Poppa nodded. "Perfect, Joanne. One needs a calm mind and to accept oneself in order to succeed in a fight."

This is stupid, Micah thought. *How was a calm mind going to help Noel against the bullies?*

"Micah, you have some boxing experience, yes?" Poppa asked.

He nodded. "I practise three times a week."

"Excellent. Show me what you've got. Joanne will be your sparring partner."

Joanne tucked her sunglasses into her pocket, hopped into the boxing ring and arranged her headgear.

Micah was frozen to the spot. "I can't fight her! She's a little girl!" he protested.

Poppa smiled. "I think she'll cope."

Micah put on his gloves and headgear and stood opposite Joanne in the ring. She barely came up to his shoulders, but there wasn't a hint of fear in her eyes.

Micah assumed the position, standing with his left foot forward and his right foot back. He brought his gloved hands up towards his face.

Poppa rang the bell to announce the start of the bout. Before Micah had a chance to react, Joanne jabbed him several times in quick succession and knocked him over in seconds.

"Wow!" Cass said.

"You're so fast!" Noel said.

Micah took off his headgear, scowling. He'd never lost a boxing spar that quickly.

"Even though Joanne is physically smaller, her concentration and focus gave her the edge over her opponent," Poppa said.

Micah nodded. "Guess I was kind of distracted."

"Let this be a lesson to you all," Poppa said. "Before you take on any opponent, make sure you are focused. And don't underestimate them simply because they are shorter."

Noel and Cass smiled at each other. They were both used to being overlooked because of their smaller stature.

"Now, who is ready to learn the first boxing move?" Poppa asked.

"Me!" Noel and Cass yelled in unison.

The hours in the boxing ring whizzed by, and, before they knew it, it was lunchtime. Micah, Cass, Noel and Joanne ate sandwiches and drank fruit squash outside the boxing gym, soaking up the sunshine.

"Your uncle's really awesome," Noel said. "If he was my uncle I'd be here for lessons every weekend."

Cass shook his head sadly. "Wish we could, but we live quite far from him." He turned to Joanne, eager to change the subject. "How did you get to be so good at boxing anyway?"

"Well, we are a boxing family!" Joanne said.

Micah resisted the urge to roll his eyes. *Here we go.* No wonder Dad was so obsessed with the great family boxing legacy.

"Also, Uncle Femi has been training me since I was five. I love boxing nearly as much as I love spy movies," Joanne said. "I can't think of a cooler job than being a spy. Imagine! You get to travel the world fighting bad guys using cutting-edge technology," she sighed.

Noel grinned knowingly, but he didn't say anything. He kept their "secret" as promised.

"What, like James Bond? I thought only dads liked those movies," Cass said.

Joanne shook her head. "There's more to spies than James Bond. Like my hero, Josephine Baker. Everyone thought she was just a singer, but during World War Two she smuggled important messages across the border using invisible ink!"

Suddenly, Cass spotted a flash of maroon out of the corner of his eye, just behind the boxing gym. It was Frank. Amidst the exhilaration and exhaustion that was Poppa's boxing boot camp, they'd totally forgotten to check in with their supercar.

"Lunch break is over," Poppa told them, clapping his hands. "Back in the ring."

Noel and Joanne went inside, but Cass trailed behind and caught his brother's arm.

"Psst, Micah! Over here," he said, gesturing towards the back of the block.

The two boys jogged over to see Frank parked up. The doors swung open and they both climbed into the front seats. Micah couldn't help but feel his heart lift to be inside the car again. It was almost like he'd missed Frank.

"Frank, how have you been?" Cass said.

"Oh, now you've found your voice?" Frank said haughtily. *"I've been trying to call you boys for hours!"*

"Sorry, Frank," said Micah guiltily. "We forgot to wear our walkie-talkie mics today. Poppa made us change outfits for his boot camp."

"It is very important that you wear them," Frank said. "It's my job to keep you safe while we're in 1985, and I need to warn you if danger is afoot."

"Okaaaaaay," Micah said. "Is danger … afoot?"

Frank paused. "Not yet. But it could be! I am going to maintain a discreet lookout. And if danger approaches, I will sound the alarm on your walkie-talkie mics. Got it?" Frank said.

"Yes, Frank," Micah and Cass said.

The boys left the car and walked back to the gym. When they turned, Frank had faded into a colour the exact shade of the brick wall behind the car. It was a perfect disguise.

16

The following morning, Micah and Cass were woken up by the sounds of slamming and crashing outside.

Cass bolted upright. "They're after us!"

Joanne poked her head into the office.

"Sorry if we woke you up. I'm helping Uncle Femi to prepare his world-famous obstacle course," she said. "It's a surprise, so don't come out here until we call you!" The office door slammed shut behind her.

Micah checked the clock on the wall. "It's not

even six o'clock!"

Cass slowly stood up, arms and legs aching from the day before. "All this boxing training is so painful... I don't know how you do it, bro."

"I don't! Dad is nowhere near as intense as Poppa," Micah said, also having a stretch. "But you've got to admit, the training is kinda fun, right?"

"I'd much rather be at the arcade," Cass grumbled. "But hanging out with Poppa is nice. We won't have that chance in the future."

Joanne popped her head back in. "All right. You can come out now!"

Micah and Cass followed her out of the office. What they saw took their breath away

The entire gym had been transformed into an obstacle course. Taut ropes had been tied across the room, punching bags hung from hooks, and a massive climbing frame stretched floor to ceiling.

"Whoa!" Micah said.

Poppa smiled proudly. "I believe you young people would call it 'totally awesome'," he said.

"Is this the same boxing gym?!" Cass exclaimed.

"Uncle Femi invented this obstacle course before he won gold at the Olympics," Joanne said.

"An Olympic champion is made, not born. I completed this obstacle course every morning before I started my working day as an electrician," Poppa said.

"It's amazing!" Micah said. "It's exactly what we need to help Noel with the bullies at tomorrow's assembly."

"What bullies?" Joanne asked. But she was interrupted by the door to the gym creaking open.

It was Noel in his PE kit, ready to start another day of training. "Is… Is this for us?" he asked nervously.

Poppa nodded. "Go get changed. We start in precisely ten minutes."

Micah, Cass and Noel lined up at the makeshift starting line. The obstacle course seemed ten times more daunting from this end of the hall.

"The course is simple," Poppa began. "The first obstacle is completed by skipping from here to Joanne." He pointed to his niece halfway down the hall, who waved cheerfully back.

"Hey! How come she doesn't have to do it?" Cass said.

"I did it last summer!" she yelled from across the hall. "If I were you, I'd quit whining and save your energy. You're gonna need it."

"As I was saying," Poppa interrupted, "after you skip to Joanne, complete the bob-and-weave, followed by the climbing frame and high rope finish. Then, I have one final surprise. *That* obstacle is the most important of all."

Noel raised his hand. "I have a question, sir. What does—"

Poppa blew his whistle sharply, silencing Noel. "One does not get to ask their boxing opponent any questions in the ring. Likewise here. The element of surprise is part of the obstacle course."

The three boys put on their boxing gloves, picked up their skipping ropes and assumed the position, ready for the first obstacle.

"On your marks … get set … GO!" Poppa yelled, his voice echoing through the gym.

Micah didn't waste any time. He skipped forwards in several quick bounds, reaching Joanne way before Noel and Cass. He turned to see them huffing and puffing behind him. For the first time, he was grateful for all the skipping drills Dad made him do as a boxing warm-up.

"INCOMIIIIIING!" Joanne yelled, throwing

tennis balls in Micah's direction. "Get at least three!"

It took him a second to realize what he was meant to do: punch the balls away with his gloved fists. Once he'd hit three balls, he could advance to the next obstacle.

"Move move move!" yelled Poppa. Sweat was pouring down Micah's face, but his competitive side had kicked in. Suddenly, his urge to win overtook his feelings of exhaustion.

He ran up towards the boxing ring where there was a rope tied from one end of the ring to the other. The rope was lined with several old tin cans.

"This doesn't make any sense," Micah panted.

"Bob and weave beneath the rope, my boy. If the tins rattle then you must start the obstacle course again!" Poppa said.

Micah ducked and ran under the rope, moving slowly and carefully to avoid hitting the tins. He felt the boxing ring shake as one of his fellow competitors entered the ring.

If Micah wanted to win, he had to move faster.

"Come on, Noel! Just one more ball!" Joanne shouted.

Micah turned. Cass was just starting the bob-and-weave while Noel was still being pelted with tennis balls.

Then it hit him. Noel couldn't come last. The whole point of this weekend was to train Noel so he could face the biggest hurdle of his life: the bullies at tomorrow's assembly. In order to do that, Noel needed all the confidence he could muster.

The future depended on it.

Whatever the next obstacle was, he had to fail it.

Micah looked up and saw a huge rope dangling from the ceiling. Below it was a giant container filled with smelly old trainers.

"Climb up the rope, swing over the bin and land on the other side," Poppa said, gesturing towards the exercise mats piled on the other end. "What are you waiting for, Micah?"

Micah took a deep breath. He walked a few steps back and took a running leap, wrapping himself around the rope. Then, when he was mid-flight, he ignored all of his instincts and let go.

"Arrrrghhhh!" he screamed, plummeting into the soft but extremely smelly bin full of old trainers. It stank of rotten cheese and mouldy milk.

Micah gasped for air just as Cass swung over the bin and landed with a thud on the exercise mats. Cass was still in the race! Micah was out of the race.

Luckily, Noel was close behind him.

"C'mon, Noel!" Micah cheered.

Noel, buoyed by the encouragement, leaped

on to the rope and swung himself over to the other side. He landed on the exercise mats, then followed Cass on to the next obstacle: the climbing frame.

But this wasn't any old climbing frame. It was twice the height of the one in their school PE hall, and the rungs on the ladder were much further apart.

Micah watched as Cass and Noel struggled to get past the second rung. They were sweaty and tired, and their arms hung exhausted by their sides.

"Take off your boxing gloves!" Micah yelled. "I thought you were meant to be the clever ones?"

Noel and Cass ripped off the gloves and hauled themselves upwards.

"Now we're getting somewhere! Just focus on one step at a time," Micah said.

His encouragement carried on until Noel and

Cass reached the top of the climbing frame. It wobbled and fear danced across the faces of both boys.

"I'm stuck!" Noel whimpered.

"This structure isn't secure," Cass said with worry in his eyes.

"I assure you the climbing frame is perfectly safe," Poppa yelled. "I have used it many times."

"Noel and Cass, remember what I said? Take it one step at a time, yeah?" Micah shouted from the base of the climbing frame.

"Micah's right! Take your time," Joanne shouted.

Together, Noel and Cass climbed over to the other side of the frame and began working their way down. In a few seconds, they had made it close enough to jump on to the landing mats beneath the frame.

"Well done, boys. But the obstacle course isn't

over yet. Remember, you have one final hurdle up ahead," Poppa said.

"What's … that?" Cass panted.

Poppa smiled. "Me."

17

Noel's jaw dropped. "You have got to be kidding!"

"I'm pretty sure there are laws against this, Uncle Femi!" Cass said. "You're, like, the size of a mountain!"

Poppa chuckled. "Boys, have I taught you nothing this weekend? It is not the size of your opponent that counts."

"That's easy for you to say," said Cass.

"Joanne, you'll be referee," Poppa said. He handed her his whistle, and she placed it around her neck with pride.

"I won't let you down," she said gravely.

"This is impossible!" Noel sputtered. "You can't expect either of us to knock you out."

"All I ask for is one good punch," Poppa said. "I will defend, but I will not land a punch. Now, which one of you is going first?"

Noel and Cass played rock paper scissors to determine who had the honour of going first. Unluckily for Cass, he lost.

He put on his headgear, stepped up to the ring and assumed the starting position. It seemed like his mind had gone blank and he couldn't recall a single tactic they'd learned.

Think, Cass, think!

Cass remembered what Poppa had said to Micah about staying focused. He had to reel in his frantic mind and concentrate.

Yes, Poppa is bigger. But you're smaller and lighter. Use it to your advantage! he thought.

★

Cass thrust forward and attempted to land a punch on Poppa's waist, but he deftly swatted the fist away.

Poppa was quick, but Cass could be quick too. While Poppa was strong, Cass had a lightness on his feet that the older, larger man couldn't replicate.

Maybe I can land a punch after all!

But it would take more than lightness on his feet: Cass had to distract him.

Poppa was blocking wherever Cass punched. What if Cass used that to his advantage?

He had an idea. Cass quickly punched the air to the left of Poppa's waist. His grandpa swatted him away, leaving his body open. And that's when Cass landed two solid punches.

Joanne blew the whistle. "Cass wins this bout!"

Noel and Micah cheered from the sidelines, but the sound never reached Cass's ears. He was too stunned that his trick had actually worked.

Poppa removed his headgear. He was smiling from ear to ear.

"Excellent work, my boy," he said, shaking Cass's hand.

Even though it wasn't Cass facing the bullies tomorrow, he still flushed with pride. He felt like he could take on the world.

"I think I get it now! Boxing is sort of like cracking a puzzle. It's strategic," Cass said proudly. "Kind of like a Rubik's Cube."

"Or a game of chess," Poppa said.

"You've got this, Noel," Cass whispered as his friend stepped into the ring.

The blood seemed to have drained from Noel's face. Gone was the chatty, friendly boy they'd gotten to know over the weekend. He looked petrified.

"Poppa, sir, I don't think I can do this," Noel stuttered. "I can barely walk without tripping over my shoelaces, let alone fight in a boxing ring."

"Noel, you smashed the obstacle course. You can't give up now!" Micah yelled.

"Let's face it: bullies will bother me for the rest of my life. I can't take them on tomorrow or ever!" Noel said, his eyes filling with frustrated tears.

Poppa crouched down on one knee. "My boy, I am not teaching you boxing so that you can face the bullies with your fists."

Noel sniffed. "Then what's the point of learning how to fight?"

Poppa sighed. "I am teaching you, *all* of you, to believe in yourselves. Because when you truly love who you are, there isn't a bully in all of London who can bring you down."

There was a pause. "Really?" Noel asked.

Poppa nodded. "You are about to square up to an Olympic champion. I assure you, I am much scarier than any school bully." He chuckled as he stood up. "Now, let's not waste any more time."

Noel nodded and raised his fists with a determined look in his eyes. Micah and Cass looked at each other and smiled. They had a feeling that everything was going to plan.

After Poppa's boxing boot camp was over, Noel said he had to get home before it got dark. He also had some last minute changes to make to his model rockets before tomorrow's assembly.

"Are you really sure this is a good idea?" Micah asked gently as they walked him to the door.

Noel thought for a moment. "Yeah," he said at last. "I think so. I don't care what anyone says now. Make sure you're in the front row, OK?"

"Wouldn't miss it for the world," Micah said.

"Bye, Joanne! Bye, Poppa! Thanks for everything." Noel waved. He turned to Micah and Cass. "You're really lucky to have him as your uncle. You know that, right?"

Cass nodded. He suddenly had a lump in his throat. He *had* been lucky to spend so much time with the grandpa he had never met – but, once this mission was over, he would never see Poppa again. "Yeah. He's the best."

After they'd waved Noel off and Joanne got picked up by her mum (Great Aunt Mary!), it was just the three of them in the empty boxing gym. The brothers helped Poppa take down the equipment used for the obstacle course, which was nearly as time-consuming as doing the course itself.

"Micah, you did a noble thing during that obstacle course," Poppa said as he stacked exercise mats into a corner. "Sacrificing a win is never easy."

Micah shrugged, but he was secretly pleased that his grandpa had noticed. "The sooner Noel can win, the sooner we can get back home."

Poppa smiled, a little sadly. "Of course. I keep forgetting that you won't be staying for much longer."

They carried on putting away the equipment in silence. Then Poppa dropped his mats with a thud. "But we missed out on *our* match," he said. "Come on. Spar with your grandpa, Micah."

"I don't know, Poppa," Micah said. His humiliating loss against Joanne was still fresh in his mind. "That obstacle course wore me out."

"Unlike you, I do not know what the future holds. And I would hate to miss out on a boxing session with my eldest grandson," Poppa said.

Micah nodded. They both put on gloves and headgear, and walked over to the ring. Cass donned the whistle chain and made himself referee.

"You'll go easy on an old man, won't you?" Poppa chuckled.

Micah was tall for his age, but his grandpa towered over him. "I'll try," he said with a smile.

"Let's get ready to rumble!" Cass yelled and then blew the whistle.

Micah immediately went into defence mode, covering his face with his gloves. He danced from side to side but didn't attempt to land a blow. If he didn't try to land a punch, then he didn't have to face embarrassment when it didn't work.

"Um, bro? You have to punch, you know?" Cass yelled from the sidelines.

"Thank you for the input, referee," Poppa said drily.

Come on, Micah. Do … something! It doesn't matter if you win or not, just do something!

Without thinking too much about it, Micah threw a right hook. Poppa swatted it away.

But now that Micah wasn't concerned with

winning, something inside him clicked. It didn't matter if he landed a punch or not. What mattered was that he had fun.

Suddenly, Micah changed his stance and began to circle his grandpa.

"Now we're cooking with gas," Poppa said, grinning.

Micah threw punch after punch, combining lunges and ducks in an attempt to dodge Poppa's fists. He was sweaty and out of breath and felt *amazing*. The match had none of the stress and expectation that he usually felt boxing with his dad. Every time he entered the ring with Dad, he carried the family's legacy on his shoulders.

But here he was, sparring with the legacy himself, and it felt like playtime. It was the most fun he'd had in ages. Who knew that boxing could be such a blast?

Micah wasn't keeping count of the punches

landed or analysing his position. He was just *being*.

Suddenly, Cass blew the whistle harder than he ever had before.

Micah took off his headgear, annoyed at the interruption. "What's going on?!"

With his headgear off, Micah could hear the crackling sound coming from the walkie-talkie mic pinned to his T-shirt.

"MAYDAY. MAYDAY. Car down!"

"It's Frank. He's in trouble!" Cass yelled.

18

They ran outside just in time to see Frank following a blur of silver around a street corner. Yellow sparks flew from his wheels and a sharp grinding noise pierced the air.

"That's their car!" Micah yelled.

"But why is Frank following them?!" Cass said.

"I am doing no such thing!" Frank said through the walkie-talkie. *"They've kidnapped me! Carnapped me! Either way, they've roped me to their car. I'm trying to resist, but it's too strong."*

"Can't you break free?! Activate some mode or gadget?" Micah pleaded.

"I am trying! But all it's doing is running my battery even lower," Frank huffed.

"Quick, boys! We can follow them in my minivan," Poppa said, standing by a van and jangling his keys.

They tumbled into the minivan, fastened their seatbelts and zoomed off in the same direction. At this late hour, the usually busy East London streets were sleepy and quiet.

But after they turned the corner at the end of the street, Frank and the silver supercar were nowhere to be seen.

"They've disappeared!" Cass said. "Micah, if we lose Frank … how do we get home?"

"We can't. Which is why we won't lose him," Micah said in his calmest voice.

"Fellas, they've taken me down Densham Road," Frank said.

Poppa did a silent U-turn and followed Frank's directions.

"Pops, can't you go any faster? I know this minivan can hit at least a hundred miles an hour!" Micah said.

"I don't think it's wise to get too close to our enemies," Poppa said. "They may have the superior vehicle, but we have the element of surprise."

"Ohhh," Cass said. "They don't know we're following them!"

"Correct," said Poppa.

As Frank continued giving directions, Poppa followed, maintaining a discreet distance behind the supercar.

"If I know this neighbourhood well, and I have lived here for thirty years, then I have a strong idea where they're taking Frank," Poppa said.

"Where?" Cass asked.

Poppa sighed as though he didn't want to say the words that were about to come out of his mouth. "I believe they are headed to the scrapyard."

The horror of the words quickly sank in.

"B-but they can't scrap Frank! He's our friend!" Cass said.

"It makes sense though, right?" Micah said. "Noelle wants her revenge for us even thinking we could change the future. And if she destroys Frank, we're all toast! Or at least trapped in 1985."

"Er, fellas? I can hear you, you know," Frank said. *"Maybe you should hit the pedal. I know I'm getting on a bit, but I'm not ready to be turned into scrap metal just yet!"*

"We're never gonna let that happen, Frank!" Cass yelled.

"No," said Poppa grimly, "we're not."

They continued to follow Frank's directions

and parked quietly on a side street. According to Frank, they were just the next street over.

"Do you want the good news or the bad news?" Frank asked.

"The bad news!" Cass said, wincing.

"The bad news is that your grandpa was right: they have taken me to the scrapyard. The good news is that it doesn't open until six a.m. tomorrow morning," Frank said.

"So what are we waiting for?!" Micah yelled. "Let's free Frank now!"

"How do you propose we do that? This is a minivan! It has no special powers," Poppa said.

"He's right," Cass muttered. "How do we save Frank without a car *like* Frank?"

Micah resisted the urge to roll his eyes. Every minute spent talking was another minute wasted. They should be rescuing Frank, not debating their plan of action. It was up to him to make the next move.

"If I'm not back in two minutes, come and find me," Micah said. Before anyone could protest, he jumped out of the minivan and walked off.

With his back pressed against the brick wall, he crept over towards the side street where Frank and the supercar were parked. He hid behind a parked car. Sure enough, he saw Noelle and Grunton, both dressed from head-to-toe in black. Noelle was shaking the locked gates of the scrapyard in frustration, but it was no use. It was definitely closed.

Micah breathed a sigh of relief. This bought them enough time to go back to the gym, find some sort of bolt cutter and come back to set Frank free. Noelle and her bodyguard had to leave some time – they wouldn't stay here all night, would they?

"They've gone back to their car," Micah whispered into the walkie-talkie. "I think they'll come back in the morning."

"You'd better stay hidden," Cass replied through the walkie-talkie, "or you're beyond stuffed!"

Micah watched as the supercar engine started. "It's OK! They're leaving. That gives us plenty of time to figure out how to set Frank free," he said.

But the car didn't leave its parking space. It just rumbled quietly, ominously on the spot.

"Hey, Frank. Are they driving away or what?" Micah whispered.

Before Frank could answer, a hissing sound pierced the air. It was coming from the supercar.

"What the—" Micah muttered.

White steam rolled away from the supercar in thick, billowing clouds. Suddenly, the supercar began to rise into the air as though it was on a platform. As Micah's eyes adjusted and the steam cleared, he realized that the car wasn't rising: it was *extending*. The tyres grew bigger and rounder, and the car elongated from front to back.

When the hissing finally stopped and the smoke cleared, Micah saw that the supercar had transformed completely. The silver exterior and tinted windows were the same, but now it looked like a double-decker camper van.

The truth dawned on Micah: Noelle and Grunton weren't going anywhere.

19

"Change of plan!" Micah hissed into the walkie-talkie. "The supercar just morphed into some epic camper van. Noelle and the chauffeur are camping outside the scrapyard."

"No doubt waiting for the gates to open at six a.m. sharp," Frank said miserably.

"If we're gonna free Frank, it has to be now. And we have to do it quietly," Micah said.

"Give us five minutes," Cass said.

A few minutes later, Micah heard footsteps coming down the pavement. He turned to see

Poppa and Cass holding a bulky sack.

"What's all this?" Micah whispered.

"Poppa's gardening stuff! He keeps it in the minivan," Cass said.

Micah peered into the sack. "Great. Just what we need: gardening gloves covered in soil and a tiny spade."

Cass grabbed the sack and pulled something heavy out that looked like a giant pair of scissors.

"You missed the hedge shears, genius," Cass said. "This should help us cut the rope."

Poppa took the shears from Cass's hands. "I will do the cutting, thank you. Let's move fast. I suspect Mr Chauffeur sleeps with one eye open," he said.

"Frank, we're coming to get you," Cass whispered into his walkie-talkie pin.

The threesome tiptoed towards the tethered car. Poppa got to work on the thick rope. As sharp as the hedge shears were, the rope was as thick as a forearm and it would take more than one clean slice to cut through.

Poppa's breathing grew heavy with exertion, but the plan was good: the rope strands frayed as, bit by bit, the shears worked their magic.

Suddenly, a light flickered overhead. It was coming from the top deck of the super camper van.

Poppa froze.

"Grunton! I heard something outside," said a voice from the supercar. Noelle. "Check outside at once."

"Run, boys!" Poppa hissed.

"I have a better idea!" Frank said, his doors springing open. *"Get in!"*

Poppa and the brothers scrambled inside the car and the doors slammed shut just as the burly chauffeur stepped out of the super camper van. If he was shocked to see them, it didn't show on his face. Instead, the chauffeur thumped on the super camper van to alert Noelle and then walked in thudding footsteps towards Frank.

"Did you cut the rope, Pops?!" Cass whsipered.

"Not quite!" he said. "Frank, you have to do the rest!"

"Righto, boss!" Frank said, thrusting the car into reverse, pulling backwards against the rope.

"Break the door open!" yelled Noelle, as she scrambled out of the camper van.

Micah and Cass looked anxiously through the window. The rope was pulled taut and snapping strand by strand. Frank continued to throw the car into reverse. With each yank backwards, the rope frayed even more.

The chauffeur thumped on Frank's doors. Strong as he was, even he couldn't defeat the car's locks.

Noelle ran out of the super camper van in an

elegant black dressing gown. "Get back here, you wretched lump! We've got a supercar and they've got a hunk of junk. So let's teach them a lesson."

The boys watched as Grunton retreated back to the super camper van and got inside. Now that their vehicle was three times the size of Frank, it was clear who would win in this tug-of-war.

"Why aren't they driving away?" Cass asked.

Suddenly, the hissing sound came back, closely followed by the billowing clouds of smoke. The double-decker vehicle began to slowly lower towards the ground.

"Their camper van has to convert back to a car before they can drive away!" Micah said. "This is our only chance!"

"Hold on to your seat belts, boys!" Frank yelled. With one final lunge into reverse, the last strands of the rope snapped. The car was free!

"You did it, Frank!" Micah cheered. "Now let's move!"

Frank sped away. The last thing Micah saw as he looked back was Noelle's furious face. Their camper van was still converting back into a normal car and there was nothing she could do.

"That was so cool!" Cass chirped. "I can't believe we beat them. Maybe their car was too super for its own good."

"Our escape isn't over yet, folks. I would bet my bumper they will head straight to the boxing gym to find you," Frank said.

Poppa nodded in the front seat. "The talking car is correct. Let's go to my sister's place — Joanne's mother. There's no way our pursuers can trace us there. I'll come back for the minivan later."

"We just need somewhere to stay the night," Micah said. "Then we can watch Noel do his assembly tomorrow and see whether it goes well or not. If it goes well and no one throws stones at him, we'll know we've succeeded in our mission."

Neither brother dared think about what would happen if they had failed.

As Frank followed Poppa's directions to his sister's house, Micah couldn't help but notice how the car had subtly changed. The sound of the engine had a rough burr to it, and the car was going much slower than usual.

"Everything all right, Frank?" Micah asked.

"Nothing you need to worry about, young Micah," Frank said.

A few minutes later, they pulled up outside a row of terraced houses. Poppa went inside to explain to his sister why he and two young boys needed to stay the night.

Suddenly, the boys heard a series of bleeps.

"Battery levels: severely depleted," a robotic voice said. Then it said it again three more times.

"Er, Frank? Is that you?" Micah asked.

"*I'm afraid so. Boys, we don't have much time left,*" Frank said. He sounded exhausted. "*Recent events have really taken it out of me, and my battery depleted far quicker than expected.*"

"Why is your recharging station in the year 2045?" Cass asked.

"*They don't have the technology to recharge me in 1985,*" Frank wheezed. "*Bit of a design flaw for a time travelling car, eh?*"

No one laughed at Frank's joke.

"*Battery levels: severely depleted,*" the robotic voice said. "*Time left until empty: twenty-four hours.*"

Frank sighed wearily. "*Just as I suspected. Boys, I have to get you back home tomorrow. Or you may never get home at all.*"

20

It was bright and early when Poppa dropped Micah and Cass at school, while Frank rested in a nearby underground car park. They walked to the gates and through the yard. It looked much like a morning at any other school: clusters of kids ate snacks and chatted loudly, and a few others were kicking footballs around the concrete yard.

"Look, Micah! Kids are allowed to eat sweets on school grounds in 1985," Cass said.

"They don't know how lucky they are,"

Micah muttered. "If Mr Rankford caught us with fizzy cola bottles, we'd have detention for a week."

Two older boys brushed past. Cass recognized the brown bowl haircut of one of them. It was Noel's bully.

"Jason, you remembered the stones? That little twerp won't know what's hit him," he said to his friend, who chuckled nastily.

"I can't stand that little dork!" Jason, the shorter boy said. "Would you believe that he refused to do my biology essay for me, Kev?"

Micah and Cass exchanged glances. Were they talking about Noel?

"He needs to be taught a lesson," Kev muttered.

Micah signalled to Cass that they should walk away, so they ducked behind the bike shed to avoid being heard.

"Bro, what do we do?" Cass asked. "Poppa's

boot camp can help with self-esteem, but it can't do much about flying stones!"

"We can't let Jason and Kev go to the assembly," Micah said.

"How do we do that? It starts in ten minutes!" Cass said.

Micah thought for a moment. "I think I have an idea. Follow my lead, OK?"

Cass followed Micah as he walked towards the two bullies. "Er, Jason and Kev? Mrs Franklin said she needs to see you both urgently."

Kev squinted at the boys. "Aren't you Noel's mates?"

Micah shrugged. "What's that got to do with the message?"

Jason elbowed his friend. "These two are geeks, just like Noel. Makes sense that a teacher would trust them with something like this."

"What's it about?" Kev asked.

"She said she needed two strong boys to help

with something inside the school. Apparently the caretaker is off sick," Micah said. "She's this way."

To Cass's shock, Kev and Jason followed Micah into the school. He led them through the front doors and down a quiet corridor lined with lockers. Luckily they didn't bump into Mrs Franklin on the way.

Micah stopped outside a wooden door labelled "Supply Cupboard". "Mrs Franklin said there's a ladder in there. Can you bring it to the assembly hall?"

"I don't know why she didn't just ask you," grumbled Kev.

Jason chuckled. "What, with those weedy arms?"

If Micah was annoyed, he didn't show it. He opened the supply cupboard door and switched on a light. It was a tiny room lined with messy shelves and cluttered with cleaning equipment.

"In you go, boys," he said. "The ladder should be right at the back."

As Kev and Jason walked through the door, Micah reached for a broom just inside the cupboard. Cass was confused but didn't say anything.

"Where did you say this ladder was?" Jason shouted from inside the cupboard.

"Riiiiiight at the back," Micah said.

Quick as a flash, Micah pulled the supply cupboard door shut and pushed the broomstick through the door handles, locking it from the outside. Kev and Jason were stuck.

"Oi! Why's the door locked?!" Kev yelled.

"Let us out!" Jason shouted, slamming against the door. But it remained shut.

The two brothers ran down the corridor and out into the schoolyard. They had made it with five minutes to spare before assembly.

"That was so cool!" Cass said. "How did you

know about the supply cupboard?"

"I noticed it when I was looking for our locker on Friday afternoon. You know, the one our future selves left the school uniform in?" Micah said.

"Now there's no chance Jason and Kev will interrupt Noel in assembly," Cass said.

"No chance that what?" A voice behind them said. They turned to see Noel, who was clutching a cardboard box containing his model space rocket.

"Umm, no chance that anyone won't be impressed by your awesome rocket!" Cass said.

Noel smiled. He chattered excitedly about the assembly and how pleased he was with his final model.

"You guys look tired," Noel said. "Did Mr have you do another round of boot camp or something?"

"Er, yeah. Rough night," Micah yawned.

They had both been too worried to sleep and had tossed and turned all night on the narrow sofa bed Great Aunt Mary had laid out for them.

The bell rang, signalling the start of the special Show and Tell Assembly.

"Wish me luck! Try to get a seat near the front. You won't wanna miss the demonstration," Noel said. "It's going to be amazing!" He beamed at them. "And it's all thanks to you — and your grandpa, of course!" Then he turned and ran into the school.

Micah and Cass joined the queue, slowly filed into the school hall and took their seats.

"The last time we saw one of Noel's demonstrations, a fireball hit the school car park," Micah muttered.

"I know," said Cass. "But at least Jason and Kev won't be able to throw stones at him now."

A hush descended over the assembly hall as the headteacher took to the stage. He gave a long talk about the importance of cultivating individual passions, but Micah and Cass weren't really paying attention (school assemblies were just as boring in the eighties). They were sitting bolt upright, waiting for the moment when Noel would take to the stage.

"The suspense is killing me," Micah whispered.

The first few people who came onstage went by in a blur. There was someone with an oboe, a roller-skating dance routine and a bizarre sock puppet act. All of them got mild applause from the audience, even Minky the sock puppet. Maybe the audience would have mercy on Noel too?

Halfway through the assembly, the overhead lights began to flicker on and off. The head teacher apologized for the power shortage, and the boys half-hoped he would halt the assembly. But then the lighting seemed to stabilize.

Finally, Noel took to the stage. He placed his cardboard box on a small table and cleared his throat.

"L–l–ladies and gentlemen," he stuttered, "today I present to you the eighth wonder of the world!"

Noel removed the cardboard box's lid to reveal a shiny grey contraption. It looked just like a rocket, except it was the size of a football and painted silver.

After listening to out–of–tune nursery rhymes on the oboe and Minky's terrible jokes, the shiny rocket did seem pretty cool in comparison.

But not everyone thought so.

"What do you think this is, *Blue Peter*?!" someone yelled from the audience.

Noel's hands shook so hard that he dropped his note cards. The audience tittered.

"Who could that be?" Cass whispered. "Do you think Jason and Kev escaped?"

Micah sat up, hoping to see Kev's distinctive bowl haircut in the front few rows. But he couldn't see anything.

Noel continued with his demo. "This is my prototype, the Rocket Riche 3000. If my calculations are correct—"

"Nerd alert!" interrupted the same heckler. A few people giggled in the audience.

"It's not them shouting," Micah whispered. "The voice doesn't sound the same. I think it's a girl."

"Wow. Noel sure has a lot of enemies," Cass muttered.

"Quiet!" yelled the head teacher. "Please continue, Noel."

"As I was saying, if my calculations are correct, a real version of this rocket can reach a target millions of kilometres away with staggering accuracy," Noel said. "It could explore the depths of space!"

Micah and Cass sensed a change in the room. At the mention of space exploration, the audience became more interested.

"This version of the Rocket Riche 3000 obviously can't leave Earth's atmosphere, but it can reach a target with pinpoint accuracy," Noel said.

"If you say so, dork face!" a heckler shouted.

"Shhh!" someone else yelled. "I want to hear what he's saying."

The support seemed to boost Noel's confidence. He pointed to the upper balcony seats in the school hall and the audience turned.

"I've taken the liberty of planting a target on a seat right at the back. To prove the accuracy of the Rocket Riche 3000, I will launch the rocket on to the target. Blindfolded."

Gasps rang through the hall.

"Er, Noel, are you sure about this?" the head teacher asked nervously.

"Totally. I'm one hundred per cent sure," Noel said.

He reached into his cardboard box and produced a clunky black square covered in buttons and dials. It looked like he'd gaffer-taped several TV remotes together into one ugly bundle.

"You see, this remote control does all the work for me," Noel said, tapping the buttons. "All I do is input the coordinates of the target, and the rocket will know exactly where to go."

"Target: initiated," said a computerized voice from the remote control.

"How is the head teacher letting Noel get away with launching a rocket in assembly?" Cass whispered.

"Because star students can get away with anything. He's probably never put a foot wrong in his life," Micah said. "Besides, things were different back then. Back now. You know what I mean."

On the stage, Noel removed his school tie and fastened it over his eyes. He pressed a few buttons on the remote and a humming noise came from the rocket. The audience were glued to the small shiny object onstage. No one spoke. No one so much as breathed. The atmosphere was tense. Electric.

Oohs and *aaahs* floated through the assembly hall as the rocket levitated. It floated towards the upper balcony of the auditorium. The audience craned their necks as it flew in a wobbly arc overhead. Even the teachers forgot their health and safety concerns, and stared awestruck at the shiny rocket chugging upwards.

"The Rocket Riche 3000 is powered by a tiny battery-powered motor. It doesn't need much power because it weighs less than a packet of crisps," Noel said while blindfolded.

"Fake news! It's nothing but a shiny balloon," shouted the heckler.

Cass stood up to find the annoying bully, but he couldn't see who was shouting. In any case, it didn't matter. It was clear that the audience was totally captivated by Noel's invention.

"Target: complete," said the remote control.

Noel ripped off his blindfold. "Did it work?" he hollered.

An older student came forward holding a round painted target and the rocket. "He did it! The rocket hit the target right in the middle," she yelled.

The entire audience erupted into cheers.

Everyone stood in their seats, clapping and whooping.

"Go Noel! Go Noel! Go Noel!" they cheered.

Micah and Cass were speechless. This was the complete opposite reaction they expected.

"They loved it!" Cass said.

Micah grinned. "Looks like our work here is done, bro."

21

At morning break Noel was surrounded by a swarm of students who were eager to meet him and the Rocket Riche 3000.

"I reckon the boxing boot camp helped a lot," Micah said. "Noel looked so confident on stage. That had to come from somewhere."

The boys tried to approach Noel, but the crowd was too big. Micah and Cass had to push through the crowd of adoring fans to speak to him.

"You smashed it, bro!" Micah said.

"Yeah, it was so cool. Everyone loved it!" Cass said.

Noel grinned, clutching the rocket close to his chest. "I'm just relieved the motor didn't explode in mid-air."

"You, cause an explosion? Impossible," Micah said, winking at Cass.

Luckily, Noel didn't get the joke.

"Make the rocket fly again, Noel!" cried a girl.

"The battery needs to rest. Maybe tomorrow lunchtime?" Noel said.

Suddenly, two older boys pushed through the crowd. It was Jason and Kev.

"How did they escape?" Cass whispered.

"We need to hide!" Micah said, pulling his brother towards the back of the crowd.

"So you think you're better than us, Nitwit Noel?!" Jason demanded.

Noel turned pale. "W-w-what are you talking about?"

"First you send your weirdo mates to lock us in the supply cupboard, then you decide to act like a massive show-off," Kev spat. "You reckon your pathetic little rocket makes you special?"

"What are you talking about? It was just an experiment," Noel said.

"Lies! I heard him myself," said a familiar voice. It was the heckler from assembly. "Noel Riche was saying to his pathetic friends that he thinks he's a smarty-pants surrounded by idiots."

There was a shift in the atmosphere.

"Who's he calling an idiot?"

"You're nothing but a stuck-up nerd, Riche!"

Cass gulped. He and Micah had celebrated too soon. It looked like Noel wasn't going to avoid being bullied after all.

"Stuck-up nerds need to be taught a lesson!" shouted the heckler. The voice, Cass thought, was very familiar...

Cass carefully craned his neck over the crowd and caught a glimpse of the heckler's blonde hair. The rest of her short frame was blocked by the crowd.

THWACK!

A pebble whistled through the air and hit the Rocket Riche 3000.

"Get him!" yelled the heckler.

Pebble after pebble rained down. The crowd were aiming for the rocket, but Noel refused to let it go, even as it splintered into small silver shards.

Micah and Cass watched in horror at the hail of pebbles being thrown at Noel, but he refused to move. Soon, one wing was hanging loose and then another. The rocket's nose was dented, the surface scratched. It wasn't until the rocket was completely destroyed that Noel looked up, his face defiant.

The rest of the crowd fell silent. Jason squared

up to him. "Do you want a pebble in the face, or what?" he yelled.

Micah and Cass got up and stood behind Noel, their hearts racing. It was a risk being seen by Kev and Jason, but they couldn't leave Noel there alone. They were prepared to stick up for him no matter what, but they were severely outnumbered. Their grandpa may have been a boxing champion, but the crowd didn't know or care about that legacy. It was three against dozens.

"Remember what you've been taught," Micah whispered to Noel, hoping that he would throw a solid right hook.

Noel turned to Micah and nodded.

"What are you waiting for, Jason?" yelled the blonde heckler. "Finish him!"

The bully stepped back and rotated his arm, preparing to take a punch.

Then Noel spoke up. His voice was calm and

clear, carrying through the still crowd. "You know what I heard? Being a bully is a real sign of weakness."

Jason stopped in his tracks, his arm still raised, his face turning bright pink. He looked too shocked to speak.

Noel let the silver remains of his rocket drop to the ground. "You think destroying this hurts me? I've got dozens of much better ideas and they are all in here," he said, holding up his black notebook. "What do *you* have?"

The crowd parted as Noel stepped over the shattered remains of his rocket and walked away.

"Are you gonna let him talk to you like that?!" the heckler shouted. "Go and teach him a lesson!"

Jason ignored her and ran shame-faced from the crowd.

"Wait. I recognize that voice," Cass said.

"What voice?" Micah asked.

The bell rang, signalling the end of morning break. As the rest of the crowd traipsed back to lessons, everyone looking a bit ashamed and embarrassed, Cass watched as the heckler went in the opposite direction.

"Micah, look!"

The boys watched as the figure slipped out of the school gate and climbed into the silver supercar As the door slammed shut, the boys heard a muffled scream of frustration coming from inside the car.

"You mean the bully was Noelle in a blonde wig?" Micah said. "Why would she want to hurt her own father?"

"She really wanted the bullies to mess Noel up. That's the only way she can save her future empire," Cass said. "Clearly she cares about that more than she cares about her dad."

Micah smirked. "Did you see Noel stand up to that bully? There's no stopping him now!"

"Yeah!" said Cass. "I just hope it's enough to change his future. And ours."

The brothers fell silent. They had done all they could.

"So what do we do now?" Cass asked as they walked back into the school.

Micah smiled. "We finally get to go home."

22

Noel was waiting for them on the corner outside school.

"Hey," he said with his shy grin. "Thanks for standing with me back there."

"You didn't need us," said Micah honestly. "You handled them all on your own."

Noel grinned. "Hey," he said, waving a fiver, "fancy celebrating after school? Pizza's on me this time."

When school had finished for the day, Micah and Cass let Noel treat them to a slice of pizza.

After all, they would be going back home in just a few hours. This would be the only time they had to celebrate with their new friend. Plus, they were broke.

They left a message with Frank on the walkie-talkie, who was thrilled to hear that their mission was complete.

"I'll see you at the boxing gym at five o'clock sharp!"

Noel barely touched his food. He was too busy accepting congratulations from the after-school crowd.

"I can't believe Noel Riche made Jason Bratton cry," one kid said in awe.

"Yeah, well done for standing up to him," said another. "That was really cool, Noel. I'm sorry for throwing stones at your rocket."

"I'm sorry too," said a tall girl. "Hey, would you like to sit with us at lunch tomorrow? I want to hear all your other ideas!"

It seemed like everyone at school had secretly thought that Jason needed a taste of his own medicine. And everyone now saw Noel in a new light.

As Noel retold the events of that morning to a new crowd for the fifteenth time, Micah kept one eye on the front door.

"Where do you think Noelle and Grunton are now?" Cass asked anxiously.

"Probably still screaming in her fancy car," Micah said. "I get the feeling that Noelle isn't used to failing."

Cass looked up at the giant pizza-shaped clock. It was nearing five o'clock.

"Bro, we'd better get going," he said.

Noel insisted on walking them to the boxing gym one last time.

"So, whereabouts in London do you live? I'm allowed to get the bus into town, you know. Or we could meet up the next time you come to visit your grandpa?" Noel asked.

Micah smiled. "Where we live is a bit further away than a bus ride, Noel."

"But don't worry! You can come train with Poppa any time," Cass said. "We'd … we'd like it if you kept an eye on him for us."

"Sure!" Noel said.

As the three of them approached the boxing gym, the boys were surprised to see how quiet it was. Where were the kids and grown-ups training? Usually it was a hive of activity at this time in the afternoon.

"What does that sign say?" Cass asked, pointing to a handwritten notice on the front door.

"Boxing gym closed today due to unforeseen circumstances," Micah read. "I bet Poppa is still tired after last night."

"But he knows we're leaving today. He would want to be here to say goodbye," Cass said, frowning.

"Hey, Poppa! It's us," Micah yelled.

He shook the handle and pushed the front door. To his surprise, it opened a little. The door wasn't locked.

"Something's blocking the door from the inside," Cass said, trying to sound calm.

Together, the three boys threw their bodies against the front door. After a few heavy pushes, it heaved open.

Even though it was still daytime, the boxing gym was pitch black inside. The windows had been covered up.

Micah groped along the walls, searching for the light switch. When he found it and switched it on, the overhead lights hummed to life. Their eyes adjusted to the sudden brightness as they took in the scene before them.

The boxing gym looked pretty normal apart from one thing: there were about fifty bundles of bright red explosives on the floor. And in the middle of the room, Poppa and Joanne sat, surrounded by yet more explosives. They were tied back-to-back with thick rope around their hands and feet. The gags around their mouths stopped them from yelling, but their eyes screamed for help.

The three boys ran towards them and tried to untie their hands and loosen the gags around their mouths.

"Thank goodness you're here!" Joanne said, gasping for breath.

"Watch out for the explosives!" Poppa said.

The boys leaped back, careful not to disturb the bright red bundles.

"Who did this to you?!" Noel demanded.

Micah took a good look at the Richecorp logo plastered across the explosives. It was clear that Noelle had brought a lot more gadgets from the future than they had. "I know exactly who was behind this," he said.

Suddenly, a sharp cackle pierced the air. The boys looked up to see Noelle, minus her blonde wig disguise. Grunton stood a few steps back from her, hands behind his back.

"Step back!" Noelle thrust her hand into the air. She held a small device with a bright red button. "Get by the door, otherwise everything blows – including your grandpa."

Micah, Cass and Noel did as they were told.

They stepped back until they were right by the front door.

"We wondered what was taking you so long," Noelle said. "We thought you'd come trotting back here after your so-called triumph in assembly today. Still, wherever you were, it gave us plenty of time to plant enough explosives to wipe this pathetic boxing gym off the face of the planet! Nice work, Cass and Micah."

"Does this girl know you?" Noel asked, his face a blend of confusion and terror. He turned to Noelle. "Why are you doing this?"

"Noel, you will thank me for this one day," Noelle said cryptically. "Believe it or not, those bullies were good for you. They turned you into the man you are capable of being – strong, brave, decisive and stinking rich."

"Don't listen to her!" Cass yelled.

"I do not like being interrupted! One more word out of you and I'll detonate the explosives,"

Noelle yelled. She paused, waiting for someone to say something. But there was silence.

Out of the corner of his eye, Cass peered through the crack in the open door, desperately scanning for Frank.

"As I was saying," Noelle continued, "those bullies gave you a fire in your belly, Noel. That fire propelled you to do incredible things. To create the greatest empire the world has ever seen. To create a family legacy."

Noel looked bewildered, but he didn't dare interrupt the girl in charge of the explosives.

Micah strained his ears, hoping to hear the sound of Frank's engine outside. But there was nothing.

Noelle paced the boxing gym. "You see, Micah and Cass left me with no choice. They've messed with the future. *Our* future. By helping you to resist the bullies, they've removed that fire in your belly. They've stolen our empire!

Luckily, I have a plan to ensure our legacy remains intact. If you refuse to step up and rule the world, then I will have to instead."

"Impossible!" Micah said. "You can't do a thing without Noel's inventions."

Noelle laughed, but the smile didn't reach her eyes. "You're absolutely right. I can't create a new world order without Noel's ingenious rocket invention."

"And you'll never have it!" Noel spat. "I don't know who you are, but you've threatened the best friends I've ever had. I will never help you!"

Noelle smiled slowly. "On the contrary," she said softly. "You will hand over every last prototype in that black notebook you carry around everywhere. If you don't, I shall detonate the explosives surrounding the man and the girl."

"No!" Cass yelled. "This isn't their fault!"

"Why are you hurting them instead of us?"

Micah asked. "We're the ones who stopped your plan."

Noelle laughed again. "Not the brightest bulbs in the box, are we? If I destroy Grandpa, then I *do* hurt you. Because you will simply cease to exist. For ever." She leaned forward over the rail. "That's how time travel works, boys."

23

Micah and Cass froze. Noel looked more confused than ever. "Time travel?" he mouthed to the boys.

"These explosives will destroy your entire family legacy. Just like you destroyed mine!" Noelle growled.

"Boys, run!" Poppa shouted. "Go get help! Save yourselves."

"We would never abandon our family!" Cass said.

Noelle shook her head, her glossy ponytail

swinging. "Oh, there's no need for all of that. Just hand over Noel's notebook and Grunton will free them both."

Noel held out his notebook. "Fine, have it! The ideas aren't worth anyone getting hurt."

"No!" Micah and Cass yelled.

"Trust us! The future of the world depends on making sure Noelle doesn't get your inventions," Micah said.

"But she's going to hurt Poppa and Joanne! His entire gym will be obliterated!" Noel said. "Besides, how do you know anything about the future of the world?

Micah took a deep breath. They were going to have to break the cardinal rule of time travel handed down by their future selves: *don't reveal the mission to anyone but Poppa.*

"Noel, do you trust us?" Micah said.

He nodded. "Of course. You're my friends."

"Then you have to believe everything I am

about to tell you." he spoke fast. "Cass and I are from the year 2023. Uncle Femi – or Poppa – is actually our grandpa. Our car, Frank, is a time machine. And we were sent here to stop *you* from being bullied," Micah said.

Noel's eyes looked like they were going to pop out of his head. "W-what?"

Noelle smirked. "Oh, come on, Noel. You didn't think they were really your friends, did you? The only reason anyone would want to hang out with you is if their life depended on it."

"Noel, we are your friends," said Cass steadily. "But the rest is true! In the year 2023, you are a famous inventor and you use your rockets to take over the world. And it's all because you got bullied after your assembly."

"No! It can't be true," Noel said, clutching his notebook. "You've seen my inventions. They're going to help the world, not harm it!"

Micah shook his head. "You wanted revenge and to take back control. The bullying made you bitter and twisted."

"Incorrect! It made you mighty," Noelle interrupted. "You had a vision and you created one of the most influential companies in the world. Look down, if you don't believe me."

Noel bent down and squinted at one of the red bundles of explosives. "It says 'Richecorp'." He paused for a second as the realization sank in. "I ... I made these explosives?"

Noelle's eyes lit up. "You're finally getting it! You not only made these explosives, but you masterminded this entire plan. At this very moment, thirty-eight years in the future, you are holding the planet Earth hostage. Even world leaders are no match for your extraordinary technology. You raised me to take over the grand legacy you began, Noel. Or should I say ... Father."

Noel turned to Micah and Cass. "She's lying, right? Tell me she's lying!"

The two boys shook their heads. "Sorry, Noel," Micah said quietly. "She's telling the truth. But it doesn't have to be this way, don't you see? You are in charge of your own future. You get to decide whether to use your powers for evil – or for good."

"I am your only child. You sent me here from the future to make sure your timeline went to plan," Noelle said.

"Yeah, and you failed!" Cass yelled. "There's not a bully in the world who could turn Noel into a supervillain. He's brave and kind. Right, Noel?"

There was a pause. They all stared at Noel, who stood there in deep thought, frowning down at the dynamite. Then, slowly, he nodded.

"He's right! I will never use my inventions for

evil, as long as I live," Noel said. "I might have done once – I can see that now. I used to feel so lonely and powerless. But now I know that the real me only wants to do good."

There was another, longer silence. Then Noelle gave her nastiest smile yet.

"I see. If you won't do what's best for the family legacy, then I will," Noelle said. "Hand over the notebook and allow me to do the job I was born to do – or your friends die. Grunton will be more than happy to assist."

Grunton stepped out of the shadows behind Noelle and cracked his knuckles menacingly.

"Noel, just run away with the notebook!" Cass pleaded. "That's the most important thing."

"I can't! She'll destroy the gym and everything in it. I can't let that happen," Noel said. He squared his shoulders. "I'm not going to let the bullies win, not this time."

Suddenly, the walkie-talkie pins on Micah

and Cass's lapels fizzed into life. There was quiet murmuring on the other end.

"Frank, is that you?" Cass whispered into the mic. "What did you say?"

"I said, move away from the door! Now!"

The boys shuffled a few steps away to leave the front entrance clear. Frank was coming to the rescue! Something big was about to happen.

"Stall her," Cass whispered to Noel. "Let her think you're going to hand over the notebook."

"All right," whispered Noel. Then, in a rather squeaky voice, he said, "I-I've changed my mind. You can have the notebook if you promise no one gets hurt."

Noelle yawned. "Goodness, this is tiresome. Yes, yes, no one will get hurt if you hand over those designs. Grunton, go fetch."

The chauffeur nodded and lumbered towards the boys. Noel glanced uncertainly at the brothers. They were cornered, and so far there was no sign of Frank.

"Frank, I hope you have something mega up your sleeve!" Micah whispered.

The chauffeur was just a few metres away. They simply couldn't allow him to get Noel's notebook. But they still needed to stall things until Frank showed up.

Suddenly, Cass had an idea. "Forgive me, Noel!" he said, before grabbing the notebook from him and tossing it across the boxing gym.

Cass had perfect aim. The notebook landed right where he had wanted it to — between Poppa and Joanne. Poppa quickly used his feet to kick the notebook under himself, so it was safe and secure.

"Got it, boys!" Poppa yelled.

"Noelle won't detonate the explosives if there's a chance Noel's precious inventions will be destroyed," Cass said triumphantly.

"Nice one, bro," whispered Micah.

A muscle twitched in Noelle's cheek. "What are you waiting for, Grunton?" she snapped.

Grunton groaned with annoyance before turning to walk towards Poppa and Joanne.

At that moment, they heard the sound of an engine roaring outside the front door. Something smashed through the front door and burst inside. A rusty red blur that whizzed around the gym before screeching to a halt at Micah and Cass's feet.

The brothers peered down. A car was before them – a small remote-controlled car that looked like an exact replica of Frank, right down to the wonky headlights. It was about the size of a small cat.

"Frank to the rescue!" blared a familiar voice from the tiny car. *"Didn't think I'd leave you hanging, did you boys?"*

"Frank, don't tell me this is your big plan?!" Micah said.

"Yeah, where's the rest of you?" Cass said.

"In case you hadn't noticed, my usual size wouldn't even get through the front door. I had to improvise and initiate Micro Mode!" Frank explained. *"Don't worry, it's only temporary."*

Noelle's tinny laughter could be heard across the hall. "Boys, you are making this entirely too easy! Dispose of the toy car, Grunton. That will ensure our meddling boys stay in the past."

"Just you try and catch me!" Frank murmured.

Mini Frank might have been small, but he was

incredibly speedy. He ran circles around Grunton, who was neither small nor fast. As Mini

Frank sped around the gym, the chauffeur grew dizzier and dizzier.

"Grunton, you blundering blockhead!" Noelle shouted. "Must I do everything myself?"

Mini Frank let out one of his rusty laughs. *"You!"* he said. *"Call yourself a supervillain? You couldn't organize your way out of a paper bag!"*

"That's it!" snarled Noelle. "You're about to become scrap metal."

She ran towards them and tried to block the tiny car, but Mini Frank ran circles around her too.

Micah and Cass finally realized what their trusty time machine supercar was up to: he was acting as the perfect distraction. "It's not the size of your opponent that counts" was what Poppa taught them. Frank may be smaller than usual, but he could still win.

Silently, Micah crept towards Poppa and Joanne. Noel and Cass followed. They swiftly untied their hands and feet and carefully began to pick their way through the maze of dynamite.

"I thought you were meant to be a genius like your old man!" Mini Frank taunted Noelle as she grew more and more enraged. She was so intent on capturing the car and crushing him beneath her boots that she didn't notice her prisoners creep out of the door and run as fast as they could away from the boxing gym.

As they ran down the street, Micah spoke into his walkie-talkie. "Frank, we did it! The plan worked! Meet us around the corner and—"

KA-BOOM!

The huge explosion stopped all of them in their tracks. They whipped around to see plumes of black smoke towering into the sky.

The smoke was coming from the gym.

24

People rushed out of their houses and gawped at the thick smoke. The sound of sirens became louder and louder.

"The boxing gym," said Joanne, looking stunned. "Is it ... gone?"

"I'm afraid so. Unless there was another building laced with explosives," Poppa said sadly. "But the most important thing is that we are all safe."

"What about Frank?!" Cass yelled. "I think he was still in the building. He's our ride home!"

"Don't panic," Micah said, trying to sound calm. "We'll go back and check when the smoke dies down."

"Er, guys. I have another question. Who has my sketchbook?" Noel asked.

The five looked at each other. They were all empty-handed.

"I thought you had it!" they all said at the same time.

"It must have been left behind in the gym!" Cass exclaimed.

"If we left it back there then it's nothing but smoke and ash. At least Noelle can't use the inventions," Micah said. "Bro, this is a good thing!"

Suddenly, they heard something. The strange, soft, purring sound of an engine.

"No," whispered Micah. "It can't be..."

They turned. Behind them was the silver supercar. The tinted window rolled down with a gentle hum. Noelle's gloating face looked out. "Surprised to see me? Apologies about the boxing gym, but it was collateral damage. Luckily you fools forgot the most important thing," she said, holding up Noel's black notebook.

"No!" Micah lunged for the car door, but as soon as he touched the handle, blue sparks flew out and he jerked back with a cry of pain. "Ouch!" he said, nursing his electrocuted hand.

"Don't touch what you can't afford," Noelle sneered.

"Where's Frank?" Cass shouted.

"Frank? Oh, you mean your pathetic excuse for a time travel machine. It's in approximately four million tiny pieces. That old tin can didn't stand a chance against Richecorp explosives," Noelle said. "Nice work there, Father."

"You hurt Frank!" Cass shouted. "He was our friend!"

"And your only way back to the future. I hope you like 1985. Because you won't be leaving it any time soon," she said. "Grunton, let's move! We have some recharging to do before we return." Her eyes gleamed. "I can't wait to tell Father about this!"

The supercar glided away.

"She can't be right," Cass said, his eyes filling with tears. "Frank – he – he can't be…"

"There's nothing coming through from his walkie-talkie," Micah said quietly. "Bro, if Frank was in the boxing gym when the explosives detonated … he didn't stand a chance."

It was almost too much for Micah and Cass to process. Not only had they lost Frank, but their home was decades away. Frank had been their only way back. They would never see him again. Never see Mum or Dad…

Poppa squeezed them into a big bear hug.

"I'm so sorry, boys," he said. "I'll do everything in my power to get you back home."

A woman in a tracksuit skidded round the corner. "Femi, there you are! There's a fire at the boxing gym – the firefighters are on their way, but you need to come quick!"

Poppa loosened his embrace. "Boys, don't go anywhere. I'll be back shortly."

He jogged in the direction of the grey smoke plumes polluting the early evening sky. Micah, Cass, Noel and Joanne sat on the pavement while they waited.

After a few moments of silence, Micah turned to Joanne, who was looking miserably at her trainers. "I guess we have some explaining to do. I know it sounds strange, but we're really from—"

"The future, I know," Joanne interrupted. "Uncle Femi told me everything when Noelle and her creepy bodyguard showed up. I thought it was a big prank until I saw the explosives."

"I'm really sorry, Joanne," Cass mumbled. "We should never have gone for pizza after school. And I'm sorry that your notebook got taken, Noel."

"It's not your fault," Joanne said.

"You're all safe and that's the only thing that matters," Noel said. He sounded oddly unbothered about having just lost his life's work to a twelve-year-old supervillain.

Micah groaned. "I can't believe we let her get your designs!"

"What sort of stuff was in your notebook, Noel? Any cool spy gadgets?" Joanne asked.

"There was all sorts really," Noel said. "But my designs are just silly drawings with no real basis in science. There isn't a laboratory in the world that could turn my ideas into reality."

"Maybe not in 1985," said Cass glumly, "but if Noelle takes your designs back to the future, the technology exists to make your ideas a reality."

"Trust us, Noel," Micah said, with a shiver, "we've seen what your rockets can do."

Joanne stood up. "There's Uncle Femi!"

They all watched as Poppa trudged towards the group, hanging his head.

"Any sign of Frank?" Cass asked hopefully.

Poppa shook his head. "Not yet, my boy."

"And … the boxing gym?" Joanne asked.

He sighed. "I'm afraid the boxing gym is totally destroyed, along with everything in it. The fire is now extinguished … but nothing could be salvaged."

Joanne let out a whimper of despair. "So what's going to happen to the boxing gym?" she asked. "It was your dream."

"It's just a building, Joanne. I will find new premises one day," Poppa said. But his expression was desperately sad.

Suddenly, Micah realized why he'd never seen Poppa's boxing gym in the future: because it was destroyed in 1985 and never rebuilt.

Micah felt a weird mix of rage and sadness course through his veins. "Why did our future selves send us on this stupid mission? We never should have accepted," he cried.

"We've messed up everything! I feel like such a failure," Cass said.

"Boys, that simply isn't true," Poppa said.

"It *is* true!" Micah yelled at the ground. If he kept his head down, no one would see his eyes filling with tears. "All we've done is make one huge mess. We've destroyed a family legacy!"

Poppa kneeled down. He looked Micah and Cass straight in the eyes. "You saved our lives! The boxing gym isn't my legacy, boys. It is simply bricks and mortar. *You* are my legacy."

Cass sniffed. "So you're not angry?"

Poppa shook his head. "No, I am not angry.

I am proud. You have shown tremendous courage. My biggest concern is making sure my boys get home safely."

"There won't be a home if we don't stop Noelle from taking Noel's inventions back to the future," Micah said. He could feel determination growing inside him. "We have to stop her!"

"I just wish there was some way of getting home again," said Cass. "Mum and Dad will be gutted."

"You can always live with me," Joanne said. "If you don't mind sharing the spare room."

"Where could Noelle be?" asked Micah. "In a city this big, what hope do we have of finding her?"

The afternoon had drifted into dusk, the sunset casting orange light across the street. It was getting dark. They sat there on the pavement and racked their brains.

Noel broke the silence. "I think I might have an idea," he said. "What if you could get hold of my notebook *and* go home?"

Everyone turned to Noel.

"Don't stop there!" Micah said.

"Yeah, tell us more!" Cass said.

Noel pushed his glasses up his nose. "Um … Noelle is from the same year as you, right? 2023?"

"Unfortunately," Micah muttered. "She must have been picked up by the supercar in 2023, just like Frank picked us up."

"And she's definitely going back to that year in her supercar, right?" Noel said.

Micah and Cass nodded.

"So, we just need to find Noelle's car, take back the notebook, and then you can hitch a ride in the supercar back to your own time," Noel said.

"Sure, that sounds easy," said Micah

sarcastically. "I'm sure Noelle would want nothing more than to help us."

"Yeah, she's not exactly going to give us a lift, Noel," said Cass. "Plus, we can't find their supercar without Frank. He may have been rusty, but he had all these cool gadgets and tricks. How can we take on Noelle and Grunton without him?"

Poppa cleared his throat. "Need I remind you that our team is 'totally awesome', to use a phrase often employed by the youth of today. You have an Olympic boxing champion on your side!"

The kids chuckled as Poppa stood up and flexed his muscles.

"We also have Joanne's energy, Cass's gaming strategy, Noel's science know-how and Micah's engineering skills!" he continued. "All they have is a fast car and a bad attitude."

"Poppa's right," Cass said, a slow grin

spreading over his face. No one gave a pep talk like his grandpa. "We owe it to ourselves to at least try."

Noel smiled. "Then our first step is to locate the supercar. Anyone have any ideas?"

Micah sighed. "How do we know they are even still here in 1985? She's probably already driven to the nearest wormhole and is fast-tracking to the future as we speak."

"Whoa! There are wormholes?!" Joanne asked.

"Yeah." Cass smiled. "I can't lie, time travel is pretty awesome ... but it uses a tonne of energy. That was why Frank was so tired – wait! Didn't Noelle say something about charging her supercar before she drove away?"

Micah nodded. "But that could be anywhere!"

"It must be somewhere with a large reserve of power," Noel said.

Suddenly, the street lights above them

flickered into life before cutting out a few seconds later.

"That's one thing I won't miss about 1985: weird flickering lights," Micah said. "Believe it or not, we have non-stop electricity in 2023!"

Noel looked up at the blinking street lights. "Hmm. They don't usually flicker like that."

"Didn't the same thing happen during assembly today?" Cass asked. "The head teacher apologized about the power shortage, remember?"

"If I recall correctly, there is a power grid located in the school's basement," Poppa said. "I was called in to fix a repair or two back in my days as an electrician."

"And the lights have only been cutting out for the past few days?" Cass asked.

Noel nodded.

"Noelle and the supercar must be hiding at the school, then!" Micah said. "What are we waiting for?!"

"Hold your horses, my boy," Poppa said. "We cannot run in all guns blazing. We need a plan."

"But we need to get moving! Otherwise they could leave," Micah said.

"Uncle Femi is right. No successful theft ever happened without a good plan," Joanne said. "It's in literally every spy movie in existence."

Micah folded his arms. "Go on. What do you reckon we should do?"

Joanne's eyes lit up. "Finally, I can put my training into practise. First, we must attack in the dead of night. Or at least after bedtime. We break a window from the other end of school, setting off the alarms. While they investigate the disturbance, we locate the notebook. We rip the pages out, but we don't take the book itself – that way they won't notice it's missing. Then you both hide in the back seat and hitch a ride home!"

"That's not a bad idea," Cass said.

"Pretty good," Micah said.

"It's absolutely brilliant!" Noel beamed.

"Thanks," Joanne said. "And the best part of this entire plan? I get to wear my balaclava!"

"I'm afraid we don't have time to go home to fetch your balaclava," Poppa said.

Joanne whipped out a piece of black cloth from her back pocket. "No need, Uncle Femi! I have one on me at all times. You never know when you might need it."

25

Micah and Cass thought that getting into the school would involve a complex series of dangerous, stealth-like steps. After all, Eastbrook Secondary in 2023 had sophisticated alarm systems, pin entry and CCTV cameras. Leaving school grounds during the day was like breaking out of Fort Knox, as Micah had discovered when he'd tried to leave for a dentist appointment.

But the Eastbrook Secondary of 1985 had a gate secured with a rusty padlock. Getting into the school was child's play.

Poppa stayed by the minivan just in case they had to make a speedy getaway. "I'm right here, team," he said. "I won't take my eyes off you."

"How are we going to find the supercar?" Micah asked as they crept out of the minivan and through the staff car park. "I say we split up into two groups, arrange a signal and—"

"I don't think we need to do all of that, bro," Cass said. He pointed to a corner of the staff car park, now empty apart from a car emitting a hazy blue glow.

It was a silver supercar with tinted windows.

"Target located!" Joanne said to no one in particular. She began ducking and rolling towards it. She was taking her spy role *very* seriously.

As they got closer, they saw that the glow was coming from a thick web of cables wrapped around the car. They couldn't see inside the car because of the tinted windows, but the deathly quiet assured them that it was empty.

"How do we know the notebook is even in there?" Cass said.

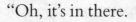

"Oh, it's in there. What else are they protecting with those cables?" Joanne said. "This is one awesome booby trap!"

"There's no way we're getting into that car without an injury. It's practically fizzing with electricity!" Noel said.

Micah rubbed his hand, remembering the electric shock he'd received from the supercar earlier that day. He didn't want to risk that again.

"We have two choices: we wait for Noelle to return and shut off the power, or we find a way to do it ourselves," Micah said.

"I like the second idea better," Cass said. "That girl scares me."

They circled the car, looking for a cable that connected to a plug of some sort.

"Look!" Joanne pointed. "I think this is where we could break the circuit."

Everyone gathered around the back of the car. Sure enough, there was a link in the cable where it could be disconnected.

The only problem? It was firing electric sparks furiously. They stood back as it hissed and fizzed. Micah leaned in for a closer look.

"Don't touch it; you'll get fried!" Joanne said.

Micah thought furiously. There must be a way around this. How was he going to get near the car without sizzling to a crisp?

Micah had an idea. He ran to the minivan and opened the back door, rooting through his grandpa's gardening equipment.

"What do you need, my boy?" Poppa asked.

Micah held up a pair of thick gardening gloves triumphantly. "Found them!"

He ran back with the gloves and put them on.

"Bro, I don't think this is a good idea," Cass said.

"Do you have a better one?" Micah asked.

"It could work! The gloves might insulate Micah's hands from the electricity," Noel said.

"Exactly: *might*. It's not certain, bro," Cass said.

"Everyone, stand back!" Micah said. "I'm going in."

Micah bent down and touched the plug. To his relief, he didn't get frazzled to a crisp. Bizarrely, the plug didn't feel hot. It felt ice cold.

He tugged at the plug, but it seemed to be firmly attached. He groaned as he tried to force the cables apart.

"Go on, Micah! You can do it!" Cass encouraged.

Micah gritted his teeth and strained every muscle in his body – finally, he wrenched the cable in two. They heard a zapping sound and everything went dark. The cable turned from glowing blue to flat grey.

"You did it!" Joanne said.

Micah wiped his forehead. "Quick," he said. "We need to move fast."

With the cables no longer posing a threat, the kids unwrapped them from the supercar and tossed them aside. *One step closer*, thought Micah. But not close enough. The doors were, of course, locked.

"Oh, who needs a key!" Joanne said. "Have you ever heard of a spy using a key? Can't we smash the windows?"

"I doubt it," said Micah glumly, rapping his fist against the sturdy glass. "I imagine this stuff is bullet-proof and shatter-proof."

"Then we'll pick the lock," Joanne said

firmly. "Have you got anything pointy? Oh, if only I had my spy kit…"

"Something pointy?" Cass interrupted.

"Yeah! Something sharp and pointy to pick the lock," Joanne said. "Don't you lot know anything?"

"Not as much as you, clearly," said Micah drily.

Cass's eyes went wide. "But, Micah, the envelope! Do you have it?"

Micah patted down his blazer and found it in the inside pocket. Cass snatched it from his hands and emptied the contents on to the ground.

He bent down and searched frantically through the bits and pieces. Suddenly, he found what he was looking for.

"Yes!" Cass said, punching the air. He held something small and shiny between his fingertips.

"Don't tell me you have a spare car key," Noel said.

"It's a paper clip!" Cass grinned. He'd never been so happy to see a piece of stationery in his entire life.

Micah had scoffed at the meagre contents of the envelope when they'd started their trip. But it seemed like their future selves knew what they were doing.

"Now this I can work with!" Micah said, brightening.

He took the paper clip and straightened it, shaping out the bends and curves into one smooth line. Then he gently inserted the wire into the car's keyhole, wriggling it until he found his way into the lock.

"Does everyone know how to break into cars in the future?" Noel asked, his eyes wide.

"Nah, Micah is just really into cars," Cass said. "There's nothing he doesn't know about them."

After a few minutes that felt like hours, finally Micah felt a subtle click in the lock. The car door released. He opened the door an inch, prepared for an alarm to start blaring. But no sound came. They had done it.

He turned to the others. "What are you waiting for? We need to find the notebook."

The kids leaped into action. Noel and Joanne flung open the back doors while Cass checked the boot. Micah rummaged around the glovebox and under the front seats.

Joanne and Noel pushed aside empty pizza boxes and rubbish bags in search of the notebook.

"Wow, this car is a dump!" Joanne said.

"I know, right? She seems so neat, but actually she's a secret slob," Cass said.

"Found it!" Noel shouted excitedly.

"Shush!" everyone else said.

"Sorry … but I found the notebook," Noel whispered. "It's got pizza sauce on a few pages, but it's definitely mine."

"Great work, everyone!" Micah said. "Have you removed your rocket plans?"

Noel was ripping page after page out of the notebook. "I'm removing everything! I don't mean to sound big-headed, but there are loads of brilliant ideas here. If they get into the wrong hands, they could cause serious damage!"

Micah and Cass, sitting in the front, winked at each other. It seemed that Noel had finally discovered true confidence.

"Listen, you'd better go, Noel and Joanne," Micah said. "And we'd better hide in the boot and pray that Noelle doesn't notice. Can you wrap the cables back round the car for us?"

"Not a problem," said Noel with a grin. "Listen, guys — I want to say thank you. For everything. I can't believe we pulled this off."

"Don't speak too soon," said a cold voice behind them.

They turned.

"Um, g-guys?" Noel stuttered. "I think we have company."

26

The chauffeur stood watching them silently.

"Run!" Micah yelled.

Noel and Joanne didn't waste any time. They scampered off in opposite directions with Noel clutching the notebook and its pages tightly.

The chauffeur didn't make any effort to chase after Noel. He didn't even look bothered that he was making off with the precious notebook. Instead, his gaze was focused on Micah, who was still sitting in the front seat. He dragged his heavy feet towards the car.

"Lock the doors!" Cass yelled. "He's getting closer!"

As Micah lunged to lock the car doors, he accidentally kicked some buttons and the supercar's dashboard whirred to life.

"Temporal wormhole located," the car's computerized voice said.

"What the…?" Cass said.

"Destination: October 20th, 2023," the voice continued.

"That's home!" Cass said. "Are you thinking what I'm thinking?"

"Are you seriously suggesting we drive a time travel machine into a wormhole?!" Micah said. "I know how to drive a car but not a supercar time machine!"

The chauffeur approached and slammed his heavy body against the door. The car rocked sideways.

"Do you have any better ideas?!" Cass said.

"Besides, haven't you been obsessed with this car since you first saw it? Now's your chance to drive it!"

The car shook again as Grunton thumped against it. He may have been slow, but he was determined.

"Oi! Why don't you pick on someone your own size?" came a loud, deep voice.

The chauffeur turned slowly around. Poppa stood in the middle of the car park. He had his fists up and a fearsome scowl on his face. A scowl that had struck fear into many an opponent's heart in the ring. Grunton straightened up and his bear-like frame seemed even larger as he moved towards Poppa.

The chauffeur towered over Poppa. But if the boys' grandpa was scared, he didn't show it. The two men circled around each other, both waiting for the optimum moment to pounce.

"We need to go," hissed Cass. "Poppa is

giving us a chance. Let's take it."

Micah didn't need to be told twice. He pounded buttons on the supercar's dashboard. He knew there was a wormhole nearby, but where?

Cass watched as Poppa skilfully dodged Grunton's heavy but slow punches. "I think Grandpa might just win!" he said.

Micah wasn't listening. He was too busy furiously tapping buttons. He needed directions to the wormhole and fast. Where was a sat-nav when you needed it?

"Where's this temporal wormhole, then?!" he said.

"Voice commands: activated," said the supercar's AI. *"Please confirm your command."*

"It's voice controlled!" Cass said. "No need to press all those buttons."

"OK, car, where is the nearest temporal wormhole?" Micah said.

"Wait! We can't leave Poppa," Cass said. "Look!"

While the boys were figuring out the car's controls, Poppa was slowly losing steam in his fight with Grunton. The man mountain just didn't seem to tire. Each punch was as heavy and loaded as the last.

"I think he's losing! Micah, we have to help him," Cass said.

"The nearest temporal wormhole is located at the following coordinates," the car said. The dashboard screen zoomed in on a map with two flashing blue symbols: one showed the supercar and the other showed the wormhole.

"I don't believe it," Micah muttered. "According to this map, the wormhole is on the other side of the school! I didn't expect it to be so close."

"Poppa!" Cass screamed as Poppa crumpled to his knees. He lunged for the door handle.

"Don't!" Poppa yelled. "Get back home, now!"

"Bro, Grandpa's right!" Micah said, gripping Cass's arm. "We need to get back home."

Neither of them mentioned that if Poppa didn't make it, the boys would no longer exist anyway.

Cass paused, then swallowed and nodded. "OK," he whispered. "Let's go."

Micah slammed the car into reverse and circled the school looking for the temporal wormhole. The last time they had time-travelled, they were too busy being flipped upside down in a talking car to notice what the wormhole actually looked like. Would it be a big black hole, he wondered, or more of a misty shimmer…?

Suddenly, everything around them went pitch black. The nearby street lights cut out, leaving nothing but the light of the full moon.

"Since when did the moon get so bright?" Micah said, shielding his face from the eerie white glow.

"That's not like any moon I've ever seen," Cass said.

The light grew brighter and began to ripple, like light refracted through water. The boys looked up through the car window to see a bright swirling light hovering above the ground.

"This is it! This must be the wormhole!" Micah said. "OK, car, take us to the destination."

"Error: the vehicle must generate minimum speeds of two-hundred-and-twenty-two miles per hour to

activate the time travel protocol," the computerized voice said.

"You have got to be kidding me!" Cass said. "There's no way we can hit those speeds."

Micah's eyes lit up. It was like he'd been waiting for this moment for this entire life. Finally, he could drive something beside the gaming simulators he loved so much.

"We can at least try!" he said.

Micah reversed the car until it hit the very back of the car park. He noticed that Poppa and Grunton were nowhere to be seen, but put that thought at the back of his mind. He had a time-travel protocol to activate.

"Buckle up, Cass," he said.

Micah turned to face the steering wheel. He took a deep breath and gripped it tightly.

"OK, supercar. Show me what you can do," he said.

Then he hit the pedal.

27

The supercar gained speed faster than Micah ever thought possible. Cass sat in the back seat, his eyes scrunched closed so he couldn't see the world pass by in a blur.

"Here we go!" Micah said. "This is it, this is it, this is…"

Just as the supercar began to lift off the ground, a mysterious object shot out of the wormhole. It was headed straight for their windscreen.

Before Micah had a chance to turn the

steering wheel, the supercar swerved by itself. The car floated in mid-air for a millisecond, before crashing with a thump to the ground and coming to a screeching halt.

"Potential collision: identified," said the car.

"What happened?" Cass said, opening his eyes.

"Something flew out of the wormhole just as we were meant to go in," Micah said. He nodded. "That's it, there."

Cass and Micah jumped out of the car and ran over to the object lying on the tarmac. It was a large black metal cube that came up to their shoulders.

Micah shook his head. "Can you imagine *that* going through our windscreen?"

"Yeah," said Cass. "What do we do now – try again?"

Suddenly, a hissing sound came from the cube. A blue light seeped through the edges.

The boys stepped back as the sides of the cube fell away one by one. The blue light filled the car park with an eerie glow.

Once their eyes adjusted, the boys could see something hovering in the middle. It looked like a sort of bulky vest. The brothers looked at each other, shrugged, then took a step closer. Cass stretched out his hand towards the object...

"Oi! What did I tell you about touching things you can't afford?"

The boys span around. Noelle. Of course.

"It's too late!" Micah yelled. "We've already destroyed the notebook. You're never getting your hands on Noel's ideas."

Noelle tipped her head back and cackled. "As if that will stop me! I have ways of making Noel talk, believe me. But I'll never forget that you boys tried to get in the way of our destiny. Your pathetic excuse for a family legacy was destroyed in seconds. Mine will not be so easily torn down."

Noelle jerked her head. Grunton emerged out of the shadows. In one hand, he gripped the collars of both Joanne and Noel. Their hands were tied and their eyes were filled with fear, although they were both glaring furiously at Noelle.

"You remember my chauffeur, boys, don't you? Grunton, I assume their grandpa has been … taken care of?" Noelle asked.

Grunton nodded grimly.

"What did you do to him?" Micah yelled.

"Grunton, have these two tied up with their friends," Noelle said.

With one swoop, the chauffeur scooped up Micah and Cass. They struggled against his grip, but it was pointless. With surprising swiftness, he tied their hands together using a complex knot. All four of them were now bound. He dumped them on the ground beside Noel and Joanne.

"Whoa. Is that the wormhole?!" Noel said, briefly distracted from his predicament by the swirling bubble in the night sky.

"That's our way home," Cass said.

"Incorrect!" Noelle said. "Your journey ends here. In more ways than one, I'm afraid."

"She's lying," Micah muttered. "If she was going to hurt us, she would have done it already."

Noelle snorted. "If it was up to me, I would have hurt you many times before now. But, believe it or not, Father is a fair man. When he sent me on this mission, he said I was to stop you without causing harm."

"Is that what you call blowing the boxing gym up with explosives?" Micah said.

Noelle shrugged. "Collateral damage. Anyway, I persuaded Father to change his instructions a bit. He said that I was to stop you without causing harm *unless necessary*. I think it's *necessary* now, don't you?"

Her face was a taunting, inflexible mask. It was game over. They weren't going to leave the school car park in one piece, let alone make it out of 1985.

"Let's get this over with," said Noelle.

She walked towards the glowing blue cube and reached both hands into its centre. She pulled out the dark object hovering in the middle, which was indeed a vest. It was made of very thick fabric. She held it aloft. A wicked grin crept on to her face.

"Oh, Father," she said to herself, "you really do love me!"

Noelle put on the vest, tightening the belt, and it puffed up.

"Your dad sent you an inflatable life jacket?" Micah asked.

"No, you idiot! This is a prototype of his latest invention: a vest that harnesses the power of anything the wearer touches," Noelle said. "I will be undefeatable!" Her eyes swept the car park. "I know exactly what sort of power to harness."

She climbed up the nearest electricity pole, going higher and higher until she was as high as the thin black cables stretched from pole to pole.

"She's going to fall! I can't watch," Joanne said. "She's evil, but she doesn't deserve to be flattened."

"She isn't going to fall. She's going to fry!" Cass said.

"Noelle, this is dangerous! Get down!" Micah yelled. As much as he couldn't stand the girl, he didn't want to see her electrocuted before his eyes.

But Noelle had reached the top. She clutched the wooden pole with one hand and reached

forward with the other until her bare hand gripped the black cable.

The current leaped and crackled. Noelle's arm shook violently, her teeth gritted with the pain of electric shocks flying through her body.

The foursome looked up at her in horror.

Then, her vest began to flicker and spark. The sparks extended throughout her body, flying from her hair and fingertips until it formed an electric field around her. With one hand still clinging to the electricity pole, she pointed at a nearby tree.

Lightning bolts flew from her fingertips, zapping the tree branch. It thudded to the ground, leaving behind a trail of black smoke.

Noelle tipped her head back and laughed, her voice now louder with a fuzzier edge to it, like radio static.

Cass gulped. He had an idea of what was coming next.

"You can have any of my inventions that you want!" Noel shrieked. "Just don't hurt my friends!"

"Your friends dared to defy me, and for that they must pay," Noelle's voice boomed, "with their lives!"

28

Micah, Cass, Noel and Joanne struggled against their ropes as hard as they could, but they knew it was futile. Even if they did break free, they were no match for Noelle's immense power. She would zap them before they made it out of the school gates.

"Noelle, you don't want to do this!" Micah pleaded. "Just let us go home and we'll forget this ever happened."

The sparks around Noelle turned a fiery crimson. They crackled and flared, the electric field around her growing larger.

"Do you take me for a fool? I will not allow everything my father worked for to be destroyed by the likes of you!" Noelle raged.

Noel played for time. "Your empire depends on my inventions. I have so many brilliant ideas! If you hurt us, you will never hear them."

Noelle laughed and the sparks around her flared. "Of course I'm not going to harm *you*, Noel. If you perish then I cease to exist."

"If you hurt my friends, I swear you'll never get a single drop of my genius!" Noel yelled. "The Rocket Riche 3000 was just the tip of the iceberg. I have ideas for weapons that could change the world."

Noelle paused for a moment, interested. "Go on."

"I have plans for robot soldiers that can cover miles in a single leap, moon lasers, hypersonic jet packs…"

As Noel ran through his list of awesome inventions, Micah caught Cass's eye. "Hey, bro!" he whispered. "Any bright ideas for how we escape this one?"

Cass shook his head. The rope ties felt rough against his skin. Grunton sure knew his way around a triple-knot.

"Typical. The one day I leave the house without my Swiss army knife!" Joanne groaned.

Cass looked up at a block of flats in the distance. Their lights flickered on and off. Then it clicked.

"We might not need the knife," Cass said. "See those lights? Noelle's vest is sucking the power out of the neighbourhood. If we just let her carry on, the fuse will blow!"

"But that could take ages!" Micah said.

"Oi, stop talking!" snarled Noelle, and the sparks surged from her hands. "I don't want you plotting anything." She turned back to Noel.

"Go on. What's this about wind turbines to create tornadoes?"

"The angrier Noelle gets, the bigger her sparks fly," Joanne whispered. "The same thing happened when she laughed."

"So we need to get her all worked up … but not *so* worked up that she electrocutes us out of sheer rage?" Micah said.

"Yes! If we can't escape then we can wear her out," Cass said. "Everyone has a weakness. What's hers?"

Micah racked his brains. From what he knew about Noelle, it didn't seem like she had a weak spot. She was tough, smart and on her way to inheriting the most powerful empire the world had ever seen. Something she'd been trained for her entire life. From the sounds of it, it was the only life she was allowed to have.

That was it!

"Here goes nothing," Micah muttered. "Oi, Noelle! Is it lonely for you at home?"

Noelle immediately stopped talking and frowned. "What do you mean?" she said. "I'm not lonely. I have everything I've ever wanted. Until you pathetic losers came along and messed it up." A handful of sparks shot out of her arm.

"Keep going," Cass whispered.

"But do you have any friends?" said Micah. "Do you play with the other kids in your class and normal stuff like that? Or are you just too busy training for world domination?"

Another flurry of sparks shot out of Noelle's hand, but she didn't notice.

"It's happening!" Cass whispered.

"W-what on earth are you talking about?" Noelle stuttered. Then she gathered herself and sneered. "I told you, I have everything I want. I love helping my father plot the demise of our civilization. Who needs friends?" Sparks flared wilder than before.

"It's working! Keep going!" Joanne whispered.

"What do you do for fun? You must have hobbies at least?" Micah asked.

"Well, no. Papa keeps me busy with my supervillain training," Noelle admitted. Sparks were soaring around her now, as though she was at the centre of a fireworks display. Behind her the lights in the flats flickered on and off. "I don't have time for fun."

"That's not fair!" Cass said sympathetically. "Don't you want a break from that sometimes? To play and mess around and watch TV like a normal kid?"

The lights in the block of flats cut out completely. The power supply was running out!

"I guess it would be nice to watch some TV from time to time," Noelle said quietly. "Or ride my bike with the kids next door."

"Then why don't you?" Micah asked gently.

"Because Father wouldn't approve. He says nothing should distract from our mission!"

"No offence, but Future You sounds awful," Joanne whispered to Noel. He grimaced.

"I think it's time you stood up to your dad," Micah said. "Everyone deserves to have friends."

Noelle's shoulders slumped and she looked down at the ground. For the first time ever, the kids actually felt a little bit sorry for her. The electric bubble around her began to shrink, and the sparks stopped crackling as wildly.

Micah and Cass exchanged a grin. If their arms weren't restrained, they would have high-fived each other.

Suddenly, Noelle's head shot back up. Her face twisted into an evil grin. "Nice try, boys."

Cass's face fell. "Uh-oh."

"I see what you're doing," Noelle said. "Trying to tug at my heartstrings. Well, you're out of luck because I haven't got any." Her voice got louder and louder and the sparks flew higher. "Why would I care about friends? I am on the verge of becoming the most powerful twelve-year-old in the history of the world!" she roared.

The electricity around her flared and smoked, the heat growing so intense that it licked their faces.

As Micah craned his head, trying to avoid the searing heat, he noticed a fizzing sound coming from his lapel. From the walkie-talkie pin. It couldn't be … could it? He looked at Cass to see if he could hear it too, but all he saw on his brother's face was sheer terror.

"Unfortunately for you, Micah and Cass, my plans do not include you being alive," Noelle simpered. "Like I said, your journey ends here."

Noelle closed her eyes and the electricity sparks flared around her arm, which was now a deadly weapon. She aimed it at Micah and Cass.

"Prepare to meet your end," she boomed.

The boys shut their eyes, hoping it would at least be quick.

But nothing happened.

Micah opened one eye. Then another.

The electric shield around Noelle was shrinking! In a matter of seconds, the electric field had disappeared completely. Noelle was just a scared kid clinging to an electricity pole for dear life.

Micah elbowed his brother. "Cass, check it out!"

The nearby street lights flickered wildly before cutting out. With no electricity for miles around, it was now totally dark.

"It worked!" Joanne yelled. "You cut out the electricity."

Micah felt a tickling sensation against his

wrist followed by relief. He moved his wrists, and to his complete shock found that they were untied. Someone had removed his restraints!

"Guys, I'm free!" Micah said, rubbing his sore wrists.

"Me too!" Cass, Joanne and Noel said at the same time.

"Don't go anywhere!" Noelle screamed from atop the electricity pole. But she couldn't do anything to stop them.

"Ignore her, obviously. How do we escape? It's pitch black out here!" Cass said.

Suddenly, they were dazzled by a set of bright lights in the distance.

Car headlights.

"Micah, is it just me or is one of those headlights wonky?" Cass asked.

29

The headlights flooded the car park with blinding light as a car zoomed in with a familiar wheezing sound.

"Frank … is that you?" Cass asked.

"We thought you were destroyed!" Micah yelled.

"No time to explain, fellas," Frank boomed. *"We have a future supervillain to deal with!"*

Joanne pointed at the electricity pole. "Noelle's gone!"

Suddenly, they heard a revving sound coming

from around the corner. They all ran in the direction of the noise and saw the silver supercar approaching them at speed.

"Get out of the way!" Micah yelled.

The kids flung themselves out of the supercar's path as Noelle generated lightning speed. She was heading towards the wormhole, with Grunton chasing close behind. He tried desperately to grab on to the door handle as the supercar sped past.

"Looks like someone was in a hurry to leave," Joanne smirked.

They all watched in stunned silence as the supercar flew through the air and into the dark swirling wormhole in the night sky. It disappeared in an instant. The only trace of their existence was Grunton, who watched in silent horror as his only ride home vanished.

Frank's passenger door swung open. Poppa stepped out.

"Grandpa!" Micah and Cass yelled. They ran towards him and he folded them into a giant hug.

Poppa glared at the chauffeur with a gaze that could melt rocks. "Run," he said.

Grunton turned on his heels and raced out of the school gates.

"Uncle Femi, what happened to you?" Joanne asked.

"That brute tied me up in the school basement! But someone untied me and I ran outside to see our good friend Frank, looking better than ever," Poppa said.

"That's so weird," Noel said. "Someone untied us too. Who could it have been?"

Someone cleared their throat in the darkness. "Um, that would be us," a man's voice said.

Two men dressed in black jumpsuits approached the group. They looked oddly familiar.

"Hey … don't we know you?" Micah said.

One of the men grinned at him. There was a very familiar twinkle in his eyes. "You should do," he said.

"You're our future selves!" Cass yelled.

"Er, guilty," Future Micah said. "We've been hanging around the last few days, just to keep a close eye on the mission."

Future Cass nodded. "We had to make sure you discovered our clues."

Cass cast his mind back. "So you left the A–Z map in the arcade?"

"And you ordered my trademark yellow pizza!" Micah gasped.

"We also put Frank together again after the unfortunate gym bombing," Future Cass said. "Micah's mechanic skills came in handy there."

"But how did you get here?" Cass asked.

"We got Frank to come and get us from 2045 after he'd dropped you off here," Future Micah

331

explained. "Might not have considered the effect on his battery life, though!"

Micah folded his arms. "If you guys were here all along, why didn't you do the mission yourselves?"

"Yeah! You could have saved us a job," Cass grumbled.

"Boys … don't you get it?" Future Micah asked.

"As much as we wanted to save the world, this mission was all about befriending Noel and persuading him to see a better path. Who better to do that than two boys his own age?" Future Cass said.

"And you two were the perfect candidates: you wouldn't have solved this mission without my, I mean, Young Cass's love of retro games or Young Micah's car skills."

Micah shrugged. "That's nothing special. It's just our weird little hobbies."

Future Micah shook his head. "That's where you're wrong, buddy. Your 'weird little hobbies' just saved the world."

"Cool! That means I can be the world's first boxing spy," Joanne said.

"But you could have just come and given us the clues in person – why were you sneaking around this whole time?" asked Micah.

"Two versions of the same person can't be in close proximity for very long. That's why we could only jump in to help now. And we can't stay long. If two time travellers who are the same person spend more than twenty-two minutes and twenty-two seconds together in one timeline, one version of us would be stuck in that timeline for ever. And I'm keen not to find out which version it would be!"

"You should all go home before it's too late!" Noel said. "I've learned my lesson I'm never designing another weapon again. Not even for fun!"

"But you'll keep inventing, won't you?" asked Cass anxiously. "Because you really might be a genius."

Noel shrugged. "I'll think about it," he said quietly.

Poppa bundled the two boys and the two men into a giant hug. "I am so proud of my grandsons, future and future future. I hope you remember that even when I'm not around."

The brothers stayed in his embrace for a long moment, grateful that they'd had the chance to meet and get to know Poppa after all.

Then Frank's horn beeped. *"Sorry to interrupt, fellas, but this wormhole ain't gonna stay open for long. 2023 is calling!"*

Poppa held them tight. When they pulled away, tears filled their grandpa's eyes. As amazing as it was to have met their grandpa, it felt almost cruel that they'd only been able to spend a few days together.

Future Micah gently placed his hands on the boys' shoulders. "It's time to go home," he said.

Micah and Cass said goodbye to Noel and Joanne.

"The next time I see you, you're gonna be so old!" Cass said to Joanne.

She puffed up her chest. "I'm gonna be taller than you too!"

"Thank you for saving me from becoming a supervillain," Noel said sheepishly. "I'll miss you guys."

"I'm not kidding around! We've got to make a move before my battery completely runs out," Frank said.

Micah and Cass scampered into their beloved car, which – thanks to Future Micah – now had plush leather seats instead of the ratty mismatched fabric. They settled in and their seat belts automatically clicked into place.

"Goodbye 1985," Cass said to himself. "It's been … interesting."

30

2023

"Hey, bro," Cass said as they walked to school. "Isn't it weird that we basically saved the entire world and no one knows about it?"

"Proper weird," Micah said. "And what do we have to show for it? Frank wouldn't even let us skip the last day of school as a reward!"

Frank had made sure they were deposited into their beds on the same Friday morning that Noel Riche had held the world hostage. They had got up and dressed for school as though nothing had ever happened.

Now they just had to see if they really had managed to change the past — and save the future.

"Wonder if we'll notice anything different?" Micah muttered.

Their walk to school looked pretty much the same. If it wasn't for the fact they'd woken up feeling dizzy from the wormhole, it would have felt like a normal Friday in October.

"You've heard of the butterfly effect, right?" Cass asked. "It's this idea that one tiny event in the past can cause massive shifts in the future."

Micah chuckled. "I guess that's one thing that hasn't changed: you being a massive nerd."

Cass laughed. "Hey, this massive nerd just helped you save the world. Which reminds me…"

He pulled out his Rubik's Cube and began turning the brightly coloured squares.

"All right, Micah," a voice interrupted.

Just like clockwork. It was Micah's friend Jamie along with a couple of other boys.

Why did this feel so familiar to the boys?

Jamie looked down at Cass. "I didn't know they allowed toddlers into Eastbrook Secondary," he sneered.

"Yeah, are you lost, little boy?" Rav added meanly. "The nursery's across the road."

Instead of going red with embarrassment, Cass looked up and stared right at the bullies. He recalled Poppa's words. *Never forget that being a bully is a sign of weakness.*

He tossed Jamie the Rubik's Cube. "If it's so easy, you solve it."

Jamie blinked. "What?"

"You just need to match all of the colours on each side of the cube. It shouldn't take you long, seeing as it's for toddlers."

Jamie smirked. "Easy."

A small crowd began to gather around the group. Jamie twisted the cube with great speed for what seemed like an age. But no matter how many combinations he tried, he wasn't even close to solving the cube. A few of his mates began sniggering.

"Not defeated by a little toy, are you?" said one.

"Yeah, I thought it was easy," said another.

"Maybe your friend can help you?" Cass asked, nodding at Rav. "Want to try?"

Rav shook his head and looked down at the floor.

"I'll put you out of your misery," Cass said. "Give it here."

He took the cube from Jamie and spun it at all angles. In under thirty seconds, each side was all one colour: red, blue, orange, yellow, white and green. The Rubik's Cube was solved.

The crowd cheered and clapped. Some of the older boys patted Cass on the shoulder. He flushed, but this time it was with pride rather than embarrassment.

"Nice one, Cass," Micah said as the crowd broke up. Rav and Jamie walked away, shoulders hunched.

The school bell rang, blaring through the playground.

Excited kids rushed past the two boys. Micah heard snatches of conversation talking about some "big announcement".

"Why does this all sound so familiar?" Cass asked.

The loudspeaker screeched into life. *"Good morning, children. Will all pupils head to the main hall for a very special assembly? Thank you."*

"This is it!" Micah said. "It's like we're experiencing Friday all over again."

Cass gulped. "This is when we find out if we

really stopped Noel Riche from taking over the world."

The boys took their seats at the back of the hall. They were primed to make a quick exit if needed.

Mrs Spencer took to the stage. "Welcome, students! Today is a very special Friday morning," she began. "As many of you will know, our very own Head of Science has just been awarded one of the highest and most prestigious prizes for science in the world for his latest invention. Today he's going to tell us all about it. Please give a warm Eastbrook Secondary round of applause to Mr Riche!"

A middle-aged man stepped on to the stage. He was wearing a white coat over his shirt and bow tie, and looked genuinely embarrassed by the applause. His hair was rumpled and his eyes were kind.

"You rule, Mr Riche!" one of the kids yelled.

The projector screen flickered on.

"Thank you, everyone," Mr Riche said. "My invention is designed to clean the oceans of plastic debris. The giant barrier sits under the ocean and filters out…"

As Mr Riche described his world-changing invention, Micah leaned in to whisper in Cass's ear. "You're telling me that he's gone from being a supervillain to saving the whales?" he said.

Cass nodded. "Looks like it. And it's thanks to us!"

"Quiet, boys!" Mr Rankford hissed behind them. Some things had *not* changed.

Micah rolled his eyes. "If only he knew we saved his precious Volvo," he muttered.

Once Mr Riche had finished his brief presentation, Mrs Spencer took to the stage again. "It's simply remarkable! Mr Riche is too modest to say, but this invention is being heralded as revolutionizing the way we approach climate change. And, needless to say, he has accepted no money for the invention but has put it all back into funding more research. A true hero."

Mr Riche turned pink at the ears. "Thank you, Mrs Spencer. But I'm no hero. It's important we all do our part in ending global warming. We all have to share this planet, after all."

"Any questions from the audience?" Mrs Spencer asked.

A girl in the front row put up her hand. "Does your invention have a name?" she asked.

Mr Riche smiled. "It does indeed! I couldn't have finished this invention without the support of my family, and particularly my daughter. I've named it after her: the Noelle Ocean Trawler! Give us a wave, Noelle."

"You've got to be kidding me..." Cass said.

A girl with dark brown hair stood up in the front row. She turned to face the audience and took a bow as they clapped.

Then Noelle did something that Micah and Cass had never seen her do before: she smiled. Not an evil grin or a cackle, but a true, heart-warming smile.

"I'm so proud of you, Dad!" she beamed.

"I guess Noelle is ... nice now?" Micah muttered. "Did we do that too?"

The assembly finished and Cass and Micah made their way to the first lessons of the day. Their classmates milled around, complaining about homework and tests. They had no idea that, in another 2023, they would have faced certain annihilation today.

"See you at the school gates at three, bro?" Cass asked.

Micah nodded. "Yep, but I need to get home quickly. I've got boxing class with Dad tonight! And then awesome Aunty Joanne's coming over! Never thought I'd say it, but I'm excited to see her!"

"Whoa! That's the first time I've heard you

be enthusiastic about boxing."

Micah grinned. "I guess Poppa taught me the beauty in it. That it's fun as well as hard work."

"You're not quitting the car designing, are you?" Cass asked.

"No way! In fact, our little trip gave me an idea for a sick supercar engine prototype," Micah said. "Mr Riche might not be the only inventor, you know."

The brothers walked down the corridor. On the way to their science class, they noticed a small crowd around Mr Riche as he awkwardly accepted congratulations.

For a split-second, Noel looked up and caught Micah's eye. He smiled briefly at the two boys, a flicker of recognition, before returning to his conversation.

"Hey, Micah. Do you think he…"

"Remembers us?" Micah shrugged. "Guess we will have to wait and see."

ASHLEY BANJO is the founder of street dance collective Diversity (winners of **BRITAIN'S GOT TALENT** in 2009), a creative director for many TV shows, a TV presenter and judge on hugely popular shows such as **DANCING ON ICE** and **BRITAIN'S GOT TALENT**.

JORDAN BANJO is a key member of Diversity and has presented **THE GREATEST DANCER**. He is the current **KISS FM** Breakfast Show presenter with Diversity member Perri Kiely.

They are passionate about reaching kids through their storytelling.

🐦 @ASHLEYBANJO @JORDAN_BANJO
📷 @ASHLEYBANJOGRAM @JORDBANJO

Photo © Tito Olaniyan

ALEXANDRA SHEPPARD is a social media strategist by day and writer by night. She is the author of *Oh My Gods*.

🐦 @ALEXSHEPPARD

📷 @ALEXSHEPPARD19

READ ON FOR CHAPTER 1 OF
FLY HIGH CREW

1

As soon as the school bell rang, Trey and Jax raced to their street dance rehearsal. Neither of them suspected that a cataclysmic, life-changing event was just around the corner.

Cataclysmic, life-changing events simply didn't happen in a place like this.

Park View High School on a Tuesday afternoon had "normal" stamped all over it. If you looked up the word "normal" in the dictionary, you might just find a picture of the grey concrete schoolyard right beside it.

Looking boringly normal.

Trey waited for his little brother by the benches in the schoolyard. Jax was late. Like normal.

Jax eventually turned up and greeted his big bro with a punch on the arm. "All right, big man?" The sleeves of his over-sized school blazer dangled past Jax's wrists. Mum said he'd grow into it, but it was already May. He looked like he'd been forced into Trey's cast-offs.

Where was this growth spurt everyone said Jax was due? He was sick and tired of being the shortest boy in Year Seven.

Although Trey was lanky and Jax was pint-sized, they were instantly recognizable as brothers. They both shared the same light-brown skin that tanned to a deep brown at the first hint of sunshine. And thanks to regular barber trips with Dad, their thick brown hair was always trimmed to razor-sharp perfection.

Trey rubbed the sore spot on his arm. "Oi!

Save that energy for rehearsal."

They made their way to the PE hall like they did every Tuesday (except for the ones when Jax was in detention).

"Yo, Jax. Please tell me you turned in your French homework today?" Trey asked.

Jax waved his hand dismissively. "I'll get round to it."

Trey narrowed his eyes at Jax. "Because if it's late again, Mr Camembert will give you detention, and—"

"Heard you the first time, bro!" Jax interrupted. "Besides, I know all the answers. It'll take me ten minutes, tops."

"Oh yeah?" Trey smirked. "Ask me a question in French, then."

Jax stopped walking. He thought long and hard for several seconds. "Ummmm. Oui?"

Trey couldn't help but burst into laughter. "Just make sure that homework gets finished tonight, Jax. We can't afford to miss you for another rehearsal. Your Applejacks need work," he smirked.

"Tyrone! Jackson!"

Trey and Jax stopped in their tracks. Only one teacher at Park View High School always got their names wrong.

It was Mr Crankshaw, although half the school called him "Stankshaw" when his back was turned. And he was frowning so hard that even his giant bushy monobrow looked angry. The deputy head had an eerie ability to sense when a student was about to have fun on school grounds.

Laughing too hard? Nose not glued to a textbook? Daring to chat during one of his snoozefest geography lessons? Then Mr Crankshaw would be in your face quicker than you could say "tectonic plates".

Mr C had had it in for Trey and Jax since day

one. He'd called their parents for everything from uniform infractions (the school jumper had to be royal blue, not navy blue) to "inappropriate" hairstyles. And now it seemed that Jax was in for the same treatment. It felt so unfair.

"Sir, my name's Trey and my brother's name is Jax," Trey said patiently. How hard could it be to remember two names?

"Why are you boys loitering after home time?" Mr Crankshaw sneered. "I don't imagine you're staying late at the library?"

Trey sighed. Here we go.

Logan, the rugby team captain, seemed to appear out of nowhere. He stood next to Mr Crankshaw and peered down at the brothers.

"Sir, one of them's wearing trainers!" Logan said. "Isn't that against the rules?"

It was one thing being told off by a teacher. But when the school bully gets involved? That violates an unspoken rule of the playground.

Mr Crankshaw peered down at Jax's feet. "Right you are, Logan. Jackson, do explain why you're wearing leisure shoes on school grounds."

"I'm on my way to rehearsal with Fly High Crew, and—"

"A crew? You mean there's more of you?!" Mr Crankshaw spluttered. The angrier he got, the

more his giant monobrow wiggled like a furry grey caterpillar.

"Oh, there are loads of them," Logan said. "They play loud music and make a right mess of the PE hall. I've seen it with my own eyes, Sir!"

"This is most irregular, I must say," Mr Crankshaw huffed. "Thank you for the information, Logan."

A shark-toothed grin spread on to Logan's face. "Any time, Sir," he said before sidling away.

Ignoring Logan, Trey stepped in front of his little brother. "I can explain, Mr Crankshaw. Fly High Crew is our street dance squad, and we practise after school on Tuesdays. Other people use it to practise gymnastics, trampolining, martial arts … all sorts. Ms Tackle supervises!"

Jax looked at his brother proudly. Trey had petitioned their PE teacher, Ms Tackle, to let them use the PE hall. Thanks to him, kids at school like Trey and Jax finally had a real space to master their skills.

Sure, it was a tight squeeze and not a session went past without a squabble. The gymnasts grumbled about the street dancers' hip-hop. The street dancers had it in for the trampolinists, who took up way too much room.

It wasn't perfect, but it was theirs. Just as long as Mr Crankshaw kept his nose (and giant bushy monobrow) out of it. If he saw how much fun they were having, he'd ban it for sure.

"Hmph. Cartwheels won't help you pass exams. You'd do well to put homework first, Tyrone," Mr Crankshaw said.

"For the last time, his name is Trey! How would you like it if I called you Mr Stankshaw?!" Jax blurted out.

Mr Crankshaw's face went redder than a chilli pepper.

Trey gulped. Jax had gone too far.

But Mr C didn't scream, shout or threaten Jax with detention for the rest of his days. His eyes narrowed. "You and your little gang are going to regret that," he said quietly. Then he went back inside the school.

"We're not a gang," Trey muttered. "Since when does dancing after school make us a gang?"

Crankshaw would have no choice but to eat his words when Fly High Crew took first prize at the annual Summer Talent Show at the end of term.

Trey didn't set up Fly High Crew just so he could do a few backflips. Oh, no.

He had big plans for his squad. Like, colossal.

And it all started with making sure Fly High Crew was the BADDEST, the GREATEST and most EXCEPTIONAL street dance troupe in town.

"He's jealous of our moves. Stankshaw must be the stiffest man in the entire universe," Jax said. "What sound do you think his knees make when he bends? Bet they go snap, crackle and pop!"

The boys fell about laughing. They felt a bit better already.

"Come on, joker," Trey said. "Less laughing, more practising."

That trophy wasn't going to win itself.